Roots & Roadmaps

The Carringtons

Nicole Linette

Thank you to our families for handling bedtime routines and moody moments as we made time to bring our vision to life. To all those searching, we hope you find your home, your roots, and your adventures.

NICOLE LINETTE

Checklist Vs. Vibes

NICOLE LINETTE

Chapter One

Indie

I ndie's red curls whipped in the wind as she breathed in the fresh spring air, singing along to Taylor Swift in her sun-faded van, as if she hadn't taken a wrong turn just twenty minutes ago. She turned off Siri's voice on her phone somewhere outside Bangor, but she was pretty sure this sleepy little town had to be Deer Isle. She could smell salt in the air, see the weathered shingle roofs poking through the trees, and most importantly, she could spot the telltale line of canopy tents stretching across the town green.

"Made it," she whispered with a grin, tapping the steering wheel. Her hands showed the wear of a tradesperson, and her fingernails were polished with remnants of her last project.

She was late, obviously, but Indie never rushed. Rushing made people sweaty and mean, and she was not about to be put into those categories. Besides, her stand always came together in record time. And if the market manager had something to say about it, well, she'd charm them with free soap and a smile. She had a habit of never making it anywhere in record time, but she always made it, and really, wasn't that the most important part? It was as if being fashionably late was a part of her, and who was she to fight her own personality?

She was pulled into the grass beside the other vendor vehicles, her van and pull-along trailer drawing more than a few curious glances. It was hard to miss a lavender Volkswagen bus with a matching lavender trailer; its paint was sun-bleached but still proud, with gold vines curling up the sides and a string of faded pennants fluttering along the top.

Indie hopped out, bare feet slipping into worn sandals, a lemon-yellow wrap skirt swirling around her ankles. She glanced up, confirming her light blue trusty beach cruiser was still secured to the top of the van. A few locals openly stared. She gave them a cheerful wave. "Hey there!" she called, as if they were already old friends. Today was going to be a magical day, as she believed most days had the potential to be. She could feel the magic in her soul, as the tingle of excitement in the air danced across her skin. In a practiced manner, she loaded her supplies into her pop-up wagon and set off to find her booth.

Indie strolled along the grass, pulling her wagon, smiling and nodding at the other vendors, who paused their customer interactions to smile at her and raise their eyebrows in return.

Some gave polite nods, others just stared, like she was a butterfly that landed in the wrong garden. The sense of ease radiated off most of the vendors, and she had a feeling they were deeply rooted in this community.

She felt a shift in the atmosphere as she spotted her booth space, its emptiness like a fresh canvas waiting for her to fill it. She scrunched her nose, feeling a wave of uneasiness, and looked for the source of discontent until she made direct eye contact with a taller, well-built man with short brown hair and green eyes. He wore a green button-up shirt that enhanced his eyes and gave a small glimpse of his farmer's tan and thick biceps. Indie found herself giving him a once-over, taking in the features of his body, but the attraction stopped at his face, and he appeared to be grimacing at her presence.

"Hi!" she chirped to the man across from her, where glossy jars of honey sat on a gingham tablecloth beside signs reading farm fresh eggs and goat milk for sale.

He looked startled, as if he didn't expect her to break the silence. "Hey," he said, nodding once, returning to his work. His discontent poured off him like a water fountain. Still, there was something about the way his hands moved steadily, like someone who knew how to take care of things.

Pretending to be unbothered, Indie pulled her small table from the wagon and began unloading her crates of handmade soaps, dried wildflower bouquets, herbal tea blends, and embroidered cloth napkins that said things like "Don't Be Salty" and "Butter Dish Bestie." She moved like she'd done this a hundred times because she had traveled all over the US, ebbing and flowing with the seasons. Within fifteen minutes, the stand was open and humming with color and scent.

And within twenty, there was a crowd.

It happened in every market. Indie didn't fully understand it—she just knew people liked to linger near her. Maybe it was her stand, bursting with color and sunshine. Perhaps it was her wild laugh. Or maybe it was the energy she carried, so carefree that it felt like she could drift away at any moment without a hint of worry.

Either way, she sold out before noon. The other vendors looked at her, envy and wonder written across their faces. It was hard to understand how this young newcomer could outshine and outsell them.

She started packing up, she was humming, cheeks flushed, and red waves pulled into a messy pile on her head. She looked over to the honey guy and offered another friendly smile. "Didn't catch your name earlier," she said, walking closer to inspect his booth and reaching out a hand still dusted with dried lavender from her last order. "I'm Indie."

He wiped his hand on his jeans and took hers, just a touch hesitantly. "Lucas."

"Nice to meet you, Lucas. Your honey smells amazing. Are you the beekeeper?"

He nodded once. "It's from the family farm."

"Love that," she said, and meant it. There was something comforting about the idea of roots that never moved. A foreign concept to someone who lived out of a van for the past 6 years. He was cute in a rugged, broody, probably-has-a-favorite-flannel kind of way, but she didn't linger on it. She'd learned not to get too curious too quickly. Market crushes faded with the seasons, and like the seasons, she too faded in and out of towns. When Lucas didn't respond, she let her smile soften before giving a brief nod and heading on her way.

Indie loaded the last of her crates into the van, then drove a few winding miles to her favorite kind of place: nowhere in particular.

Her campsite was a patch of grass and gravel at the edge of a wooded bluff. There was a fire pit ringed in stones, a picnic table starting to grow moss, and most importantly, a postcard view of the water. She parked her van, kicked off her shoes, and stretched like a cat in the late afternoon sun. The grass and gravel on her feet were the only things that ever made her feel rooted. The hum of bugs, the scent of pine, the faint clang of a distant bell buoyed it all, whispering: stay a little while.

She pulled her map from the glove box, holding it against the van as she surveyed the peninsula's farmers' market loop. She set up her hammock, pulled the crates out, and started sorting through what little stock she had left, making notes in her messy little logbook. The farmers' market season had just begun, and Indie would need to resupply if she was to continue to participate. She planned to do the Brooklin market, Stonington, and the Blue Hill market. Then again, if she woke tomorrow and had the urge to move on out of Maine, she would.

She brewed a cup of mint tea over the camp stove and curled up in her hammock after stocking the fire. With her embroidery hoop and audiobook playing softly in the background, a cozy kind of silence settled around her.

She didn't know how long she'd stay, or if this town would feel like something she could hold onto. But for now, the air smelled like pine and saltwater, her fingers were busy, and her heart was light.

And that was more than enough.

Chapter Two

Lucas

The town of Deer Isle still held its breath in May. Morning mist clung to the empty stalls at the park as a single truck pulled up. Through his windshield, Lucas observed locals strolling with their dogs along the path. Soon, vendors would flock from their farms, kitchens, and work. Tables to fill the space with fresh greens, eggs, local honey, wildflower bouquets, and homemade jams. He could feel the pulse of the market beneath the surface, his thoughts circling one burning question: What was in store for him this season? He turned his truck on and reversed from his spot, heading back to his own farm and the chatter of his family. Tomorrow, he would relive his childhood running the family stand for the first time in a decade.

Lucas arrived as soon as the sun peeked over the horizon to set up the family stand. He carefully placed his signs and inspected each canister of goat milk, carton of eggs, and jar of honey. Soon, his products would include produce from his mother's garden, and on that day, he too would inspect every piece before placing it out with care. He was diligent and precise in his maneuvers, as if he had set the stand up hundreds of times because, in fact, he had. His family farm rested a short distance from the market, and he felt like he could hear the hustle and bustle of his family starting on their daily chores as he set up their booth.

He took in a deep breath, tasting the salt in the air on his tongue, and he was ready. However, the booth next to him sat empty. Lucas was on time, if not early, he believed in being responsible and upholding the commitments you make. The irresponsibility of the vendor of this empty spot created a knot of disgust and anxiety in the pit of his stomach.

As if he spoke her into existence, a slender woman with flowing auburn hair strolled down the aisle, pulling an overflowing cart. He watched her stop at the empty spot. "Hi," she chirped, giving her head a toss, the sun catching her green eyes and throwing glitter into them. He felt his voice catch in his throat.

"Hey," is all he managed before his pulse started pounding in his ear, and he had to turn his attention back to his work. She was a marvelous sight, but her tardiness soured his stomach. Lucas was prompt. He believed in giving his tasks his full attention, and that started with being on time.

As the minutes dragged on, Lucas found it hard to keep his eyes from drifting over to the booth. He was in disbelief at the chaos of her setup: one small wood table and exposed crates littered the space. A variety of colors and smells seemed to burst from every inch. She didn't even have a tent. The sun seemed so captivated by her presence that it danced around her, like it was designed to highlight her slyly.

Outside of being prompt, Lucas believed in order. In structure. He liked predictability, and everything about this woman screamed flighty.

While her carefree presence at the market stirred all the wrong feelings, it worked for her. Customers gravitated to her chaos, laughing and engaged. Not a single one left empty-handed. Two men even gave her slips of paper, most likely with their phone numbers. He wondered what it would be like to give her his number... or even to have her give him hers. He shoved the thoughts out of his mind and returned his focus to his work.

Lucas made small talk with the locals as they picked up their usual orders. His family was sixth-generation farmers on Deer Isle, and the markets had become predictable and comforting for him. He didn't even typically run the markets, but his sister Charlotte and her family negotiated for the season off. Something about this being his niece Olivia's last summer before starting school: thus, the job fell to the only other Carrington child: him.

In a lull of customers, Lucas let himself take a longer glance over at the woman. He stared in disbelief, as if he had just experienced whiplash; she was packing up. She looked up, made eye contact, and flashed him a smile.

"Didn't catch your name earlier," she said, walking closer to inspect his booth and reaching out a hand still dusted with dried lavender from her last order. "I'm Indie."

He wiped his hand on his jeans and took hers hesitantly, confusion creasing his brow. What kind of name was Indie? "Lucas," he murmured, fighting back the urge to ask how she was already out of product and where her name came from, it did not seem like a normal name.

"Nice to meet you, Lucas. Your honey smells amazing. Are you the beekeeper?"

He felt as though she was soaking in his space, her eyes glancing over his items. He nodded once. "It's from the family farm."

He almost offered her a sample, but she chirped out, "Love that," and he felt a shock ripple through him.

She paused for a brief moment, as if waiting for him to respond, and when he didn't, she just flashed a smile and went on her way. Just as she arrived, she was gone, taking the sun with her. All that was left was the scent of lavender lingering on his hand.

Lucas rolled up to his house, the relief of accomplishing the first market of the season washing over him. But all evening, while he was packing up, the empty spot across from him brought images of Indie. He wondered if she was calling those men, or maybe she was already out with one of them. He shook his head. He had to get her out of his mind. He couldn't even say a whole sentence around her. And she was late. She was so late to an event that it was potentially work.

He let out a sigh, running a hand down his face. He was going to go to his house, have a beer, and forget her. He'd probably never see her again anyway.

NICOLE LINETTE

Wobbles & Wonder

NICOLE LINETTE

Chapter Three

Lucas

Lucas pulled his truck up in front of the main house. Unexpectantly, he was the last one to arrive. He spent all night tossing and turning, reliving yesterday's market mixed with childhood memories of running through the space, feeling a rush of freedom. He woke up confused that sense of freedom did not belong in those memories. He'd always been focused, observant, attached to his parents' sides while his sister ran free through the aisle of vendors.

The feeling slowed his usual farm routine. He'd mucked the stalls twice just to double-check them, rinsed the water pails more times than needed. He found himself questioning whether his memories had been tinted by last night's dreams. He gave his head a final shake and climbed out of the truck.

He could hear his niece, Olivia, squealing with delight from the backyard, probably chasing their current house pet, Otis, the three-legged baby goat. He grabbed the wooden stick horse he'd made for Olivia out of the back and headed inside.

Lucas's childhood home had been in the family for five generations. His grandmother had passed away last year, leaving the property to his parents. It was a simple, weathered two-story structure with white clapboard siding faded from time. Repainting it sat near the top of Lucas's long list of projects. The roof was pitched and clad in dark shingles, bearing a sturdy brick chimney. The porch wrapped around to the back of the house and had recently been updated with new rocking chairs and small side tables.

Inside, the hardwood floors creaked beneath his boots as he made his way to the kitchen, a mix of mismatched cupboards and newer appliances. It had been easier to make updates since his grandparents passed, but there were still things they'd never part with, like the small wood stove nestled in the corner of the current living room.

"Lucas," his mother beamed as if she didn't see him almost every day. She reached up, pinching his cheek.

"Everyone's outside with Otis, Dad's on the Blackstone. I'm just finishing up the fruit salad. Here, grab the mimosas and take them out." Lucas tucked the horse under his arm and grabbed the pitcher of orange juice and the champagne bottles.

Out back, his father was pulling pancakes, eggs, and bacon off the griddle and plating them for the table. He glanced up and spotted Lucas.

"Aah, there he is. Nice of you to finally show up," he joked, glancing at his watch.

Daniel, his brother-in-law, leaned against the railing, smoking a cigarette and watching Olivia and Charlotte lure Otis around the yard with snacks.

"Hey, kiddo," Lucas called, setting down the drinks and wiggling the stick horse. "Look what I finished, rainbow mane and all."

Olivia turned to him, pure joy beaming from her face as she barreled toward him.

"I'm naming it Sparkle," she squealed, snatching it from his hands and galloping around the deck until Daniel shooed her to her breakfast seat.

"You spoil her," Daniel muttered, stubbing his cigarette out on the railing. Lucas gritted his teeth as Daniel dropped the bud into the old coffee tin they kept out there for him.

"Oh, that's his job." Charlotte laughed, joining them at the table as their mother came out with fruit salad.

"Food's on!" Their mom clapped, taking her seat next to their dad near the head of the table. Lucas sat across from

Charlotte and next to Olivia, who was now five and demanded her own chair across from her father instead of being smooshed between her parents.

"So how was the market running yesterday?" Charlotte asked, dishing up Daniel's plate before her own. Lucas helped Olivia with hers, then filled his own before sitting down.

"Seemed pretty normal, a lot of the same vendors that have always been there. There was a new girl. She had soap and dried flowers. I think her name was Indie. But outside that, nothing too new or different," he said, taking a bite of food.

"Oh, I think I saw her pull into town. She's in a purple van pulling a trailer. She's cute and feels..." she paused, "well, I'm not sure what the appropriate word would be."

"Free," Lucas mumbled, feeling heat crawl up his neck. "I mean, um... seems like she might live in that vehicle monstrosity of hers. Going where she wants."

"Sounds like you have a crush." Charlotte laughed, pointing her fork at him. "Look at how much you're blushing." Her smile was big and wholesome. Lucas could feel the heat rise to his cheeks as he avoided to make eye contact with his sister.

"Sounds like trouble to me," his father said. You can't get anywhere in life without putting your roots down. Like I always say, nothing grows without a stable foundation, and at the root of that is your roots."

The whole table groaned, and Olivia mouthed the words along with her grandfather.

It was Hank Carrington's favorite line. He was a burly man who'd aged well with dark brown hair speckled with white, a thick white beard, and a booming voice that could carry over a field. He believed in hard work, early mornings, and history-proven methods. He also thought his jokes were funnier than they were. Hank was a respected man in the community. When he talked, people listened, and when people needed him, he was there.

Lucas's mother, Josephine, sat across from him. Her once-dark curls had turned silver years ago, something she liked to blame on her children. Her soft brown eyes and petite frame didn't fool anyone—she could throw hay bales and wrangle a rogue calf just as well as any man, though she never bragged about it.

"I think she sounds lovely," Josephine said, spearing a strawberry. Rebecca, you know my friend from the salon said that the soap she sold worked wonders on her skin after one use! And Robert from across the bridge said she sold out before noon. She must be a good businesswoman."

"Sounds like she doesn't keep enough stock to me," Hank grunted, mouth full of pancakes.

"I wanna meet her!" Olivia announced, digging blueberries out of her bowl with sticky fingers. "She sounds pretty. I want more pretty people."

"Are you saying I'm not beautiful?" Lucas asked with a mock gasp, pretending to flip imaginary hair. "I see how it is. I made you a pony, and now I'm dog food."

"No! You're the prettiest," Olivia screeched, launching from her chair into Lucas's lap, nearly spilling his mimosa. He chuckled, catching her mid-jump, and glanced over at Daniel, who was scowling.

"Men are handsome, not pretty," Daniel muttered, eyes still on his plate.

No one countered his remark, so Lucas ignored it and waved a piece of bacon in front of Olivia to try to catch it with her mouth.

"Okay, you two, what have I said about playing at the table?" Hank said, but he was grinning, waving his own piece of bacon just as Otis leapt out of nowhere, grabbed it from his hand, and hobbled with all his energy across the yard.

"No! You're a veg-meteer!" Olivia screamed, sprinting after the goat, her mother trailing behind.

The table erupted in laughter, and whatever was left of Lucas's earlier restlessness melted into the morning sun.

After chasing down their house goat and cleaning up breakfast, the family parted ways for the day. Charlotte and her crew were headed into town for new summer clothes. Hank and Josephine were checking in with the farmhands. That left Lucas to his own tasks, which, this morning, felt strangely unimportant.

He couldn't shake his father's comment. Maybe Indie didn't sell out because demand was high; perhaps she just didn't have much to begin with. Maybe she'd shown up late, unpacked slowly, and didn't plan. That kind of bugged him.

But then again... when he was a kid, if the market didn't go well, their parents would sometimes let him and Charlotte run a booth the next day at the smaller Sunday market just up the road. A chance to try again. He wondered if she'd do the same.

Before he knew it, Lucas had climbed into his truck and was parking near town again, strolling toward the smaller market.

It felt like time slowed when he looked up the road and saw her.

Indie.

Cruising on a light blue beach cruiser, with hair fanning behind her like a flame. The wind caught her skirt, the sun lit her face, and Lucas was pretty sure his mouth fell open. The van had been a reflection of her personality, but this? This was her, unfiltered.

Then clank. The chain slipped. Her front tire hit a bump. And she flew.

"Indie!" he shouted, boots already pounding the pavement toward her, a need to protect snapping through his chest so suddenly it felt primal.

Chapter Four

Indie

Indie stretched out and opened her eyes, taking in her camper. She never tired of waking to the view. Glow-in-the-dark stars stretched across her ceiling, and Bambi, her rose-haired tarantula's terrarium, was the masterpiece. She had carefully crafted and researched every piece of the tank to give it bohemian vibes while perfectly meeting Bambi's needs.

Bambi was her constant companion. She had traveled all across the U.S. with her through the highs, lows, heartbreaks, and hellos. For years, Bambi had been the only living creature Indie could count on.

"Hey girl," she whispered, glancing around the tank until she spotted her furry friend.

"Why don't I ride into town and get you a buggy treat?" she cooed, pulling her hair up into a braid. With that, the plan was to ride into town, do some exploring, hit the pet shop, then come back and work on her next batch of dried flower wreaths.

It didn't take long for Indie to ride her sky-blue beach cruiser into town. The ride was gorgeous, the salty sea air wrapped around her like a scarf, and the patchy sunlight flickered through the trees, casting stained-glass patterns across the road. She fought the urge to outstretch her arms and soak in the warmth like she used to as a kid.

Too soon, she was at the grocery store. She climbed off her bike, feeling no need to lock it up. She grabbed her reusable totes and walked inside.

The brisk chill of the air conditioning crawled over her skin, raising goosebumps. She grabbed a cart and slowly moved up and down the aisles, letting the snacks "speak to her," grabbing anything that caught her eye: freeze-dried mango, kettle chips, gummy worms.

When she turned the corner into the pet aisle, she spotted a woman looking forlorn. Her short brown hair bounced as she shook her head, her bangs brushing just over her furrowed brows.

"Why is this so hard?" the woman whined, crossing her arms over her chest, which Indie noted only emphasized the already eye-catching cleavage peeking from her tank top. Indie glanced down at her own, smaller chest.

What was it that the school kids used to tease her with? Of course, she was environmentally friendly; she'd been conserving her curves since birth. She shook the memory away and returned her gaze to the woman.

"Um, do you need some help?" she asked, stepping closer. The woman in her heels felt like she towered above her, but it was realistically only a couple of inches.

"I've given up on finding my soulmate, so now I'm trying to find my soul pet. Why are there so many options?" the woman burst out, turning toward Indie, eyes glistening with tears.

"Oh, I'm... sorry," she stammered, surprised. She looked around at the pet supplies. "I'm not sure if the pet aisle in a grocery store is going to help you find your soul pet."

"It's this stupid small town." She gave her foot a small stomp, her heel making a clicking sound. Indie stifled a small laugh, and the sound contrasted with her forlorn disposition. "I can't just go look at pets, so now I'm staring at bags of dog and cat food, waiting for something to call to me," she groaned. "I'm sorry. There are just so many options. I'm fine. I'm fine."

She pulled a cloth from her pocket and dabbed her eyes. Then she looked at Indie again, and like someone flipped a light switch, she broke into a wide grin.

"Oh! You're the girl with the soap in the purple van!" she squealed.

"Sounds like my reputation precedes me," Indie smiled, reaching out a hand over the shopping cart. "Hi, I'm Indie."

"I'm Sloane. I'm so excited to meet you!" Sloane grabbed Indie's hand, shaking it with both of hers.

"So, Sloane... you're staring at pet food in hopes of figuring out if you're a dog or cat person?" Indie grinned.

Sloane let out a boisterous laugh, but Indie could hear her swallowing back the tears. "Yeah, pretty much. Pathetic, right?"

"Not at all. But let me tell you, there are so many more amazing options than just cats and dogs." Indie glanced around. There was no way she was finding Bambi a treat here. She'd have to search the woods later.

"Oh, you sound like someone who has a fun pet. Let me guess..." Sloane looked her up and down, pursing her lips. "Are you a lizard owner?" She shuddered with mock disgust.

Indie laughed. "No, but close-ish. I have a tarantula named Bambi. All I'm saying is maybe a trip to a real pet store, or rescue is going to help you more than staring at cat food." She winked and crinkled her nose.

"You're right. That's what I'm going to have to do. I think Ellsworth has one. Oh! That would make the perfect girls' trip.

Let's do it. Let me get my card." She dabbed her eye with her cloth one last time before putting the cloth in her pocket.

Sloane spun around to grab her purse from the floor, where she'd apparently dropped it during her mini meltdown. Indie's eyes widened slightly as Sloane bent over, her black leather skirt leaving very little to the imagination.

Sloane caught her stare. "Yeah, I know. It might be a little short—but today's about style." She handed Indie a business card that read:

Pose and Petal — Yoga Brought to You.

"You're not too bad yourself," Sloane added, reaching for Indie and gently pinching a piece of her dress. "If we added a cinched waist to this... and maybe took the shoulder straps off? Girl, you're gorgeous. You've got to show those curves off."

Then, as if realizing she'd crossed a line, she stepped back, face flushing.

"I'll keep that in mind," Indie said with a laugh, pulling a scrap of paper and pen out of her purse and scribbling down her number.

Sloane took it eagerly and immediately pulled out her phone, dialing it. Indie's phone started ringing, "Walking on Sunshine" blaring through the grocery store.

Indie answered with a grin. "This is Indie."

"Hey girl, this is Sloane. Just wondering if you want to get some drinks later."

They both laughed.

"That sounds like a wonderful plan," Indie said, hanging up.

"It was great to meet you, Indie. I should probably exit the pet food aisle before the staff starts to get concerned." Sloane laughed lightly and gave a little wave. "Talk to you soon."

Indie blinked, chuckled to herself, and shook her head. She had a feeling she was going to like Sloane.

Indie pedaled hard, the bags of groceries strapped to the back of her bike. The wind tugged at her hair as she coasted down the street. Her sundress fluttered around her knees, and the sound of a nearby musician filled the air, drowning out the hum of her tires. She smiled to herself, the sun warming her back.

But then—clank.

A sharp metallic snap shattered the moment. Her feet spun uselessly as the chain popped free from the gears. Before she could steady herself, the bike wobbled, and it was too late to change course; she tumbled.

Her knees hit the pavement first, followed by her palms skidding across the concrete. The bike clattered beside her, groceries spilling like runaway marbles across the sidewalk.

She hissed in pain, rolling to sit on her butt and examining the damage. Blood oozed from her knees, and gravel was embedded in her palms.

"Indie!?" a concerned voice called, heavy work boots pounding toward her.

She looked up, squinting at the sunlit silhouette of Lucas, the honey guy from yesterday's market.

"Oh, you remember my name." She tried to laugh, holding back the wave of pain as she attempted to get up and gather her groceries.

"No one could forget your name," he said gently, holding out his hand to help her up. Then he crouched down. "That was a nasty fall. Let me see."

He brushed her dress up slightly, exposing her knees. His hands grazed her skin, sending a wave of heat through her.

"Oh, um—it's okay, just a slight fall," she said quickly, closing her hands to hide her scraped palms.

"You're bleeding... blood," he said softly, the words cradling her. Lucas wasn't afraid of blood, years on the farm ironed that fear out of him, but he did have a fear of others being hurt. He hated to see pain on their faces, and the tremble in their hands; even small incidents caused him to lead into action. He looked up at her, emerald eyes sparkling with concern.

She laughed nervously. "Well, it'd be crazy if it were anything else."

A buzz came from her pocket. She jumped slightly and fished out her phone, a text from Sloane.

> Hey girl, you okay?

> I saw the crash, and Lucas (heart eyes) came running to the rescue.

> Girl, I've never seen him move so fast. I need deets. Let's plan to get drinks soon (kiss face, kiss face).

Indie chuckled, momentarily forgetting that Lucas was still crouched in front of her. He cleared his throat, and she looked down, her face warming.

"Oh... oh, sorry, really I'm okay," she said.

Lucas stood, and she had to tilt her head back to look up at him—he was tall. Her head barely reached his shoulder.

"Oh, you definitely work the farm," she murmured, eyes trailing up his solid frame.

He was smirking, clearly aware she was checking him out.

"Well, I wouldn't be a decent human if I didn't help you gather your..." he glanced at the mess, "... groceries."

Indie looked down, another wave of heat rushing through her when her eyes landed on a bright pink box of tampons lying on the sidewalk.

"I-uh—" she stammered, stepping quickly around the bike to snatch up the box.

Lucas laughed—a deep, full sound—and walked past her, scooping the scattered items into her tote. "Nothing to be embarrassed about, I've bought the same ones before." Then he picked up the bike, eyeing the chain.

"My truck's just there," he said, pointing behind him. But when he noticed she hadn't moved, he frowned and stepped closer.

"Come on," he said softly, slipping his free hand under her elbow and giving a slight nudge.

"I can walk," she said, breaking out of her daze. "Really. It's not far, and I'm okay."

But she wasn't sure that was true. She had a strange feeling that if she got into that truck, she might never want to leave.

"Nope. I won't take no for an answer. Come on."

He led the way, and Indie followed, trailing slightly behind, her eyes completely and shamelessly glued to his butt and tight muscles under his T-shirt.

"I can feel you staring at my butt," he said over his shoulder, opening the tailgate.

Indie bit her lip, stifling a laugh. She was definitely going to burst into flames at this rate.

She climbed into the truck, thankful he didn't offer to help her in. Though she could still feel the lingering warmth from where his hand had brushed her leg earlier.

"Thanks for the drive back," she said bashfully, returning to her usual bubbly self.

"Well, we wouldn't want your popsicles to melt. But I wish you'd let me get the med kit and clean up those knees. And your hands." He glanced over at her as he drove.

"Oh, no worries. I'll clean up at home. Easy peasy. I've got a good antibacterial soap bar I've been working on. This is the perfect chance to test it out."

He was quiet for a moment, thoughtful. "Did you not pack much merchandise?"

It took her a second to connect the dots. "Oh, from leaving the market early? No, I sold out. Your town's clearly craving something new," she teased.

But a shadow passed over Lucas's face.

"It has been a while since we had anything new," he said quietly as he turned onto the road toward her campsite.

"I didn't mean it as an insult," she offered quickly. "I usually sell out pretty fast. I just try not to overstock—I'd rather do more markets and spread the love than haul unsold stuff back into the van."

He hummed, seeming to turn that over in his head. "That makes sense. Let me help you with your stuff," Lucas said after parking the truck.

He walked around to the back of the truck while she jumped down and opened her trailer. Lucas lowered the bike and immediately started fiddling with the chain.

"You might need a new one," he called as she ducked her head inside the trailer.

"Okay. I think I have a spare, actually," she called back. When she turned to leave the trailer, she nearly crashed into him.

He was standing just inside, looking around.

"Have you ever been in a travel trailer before?" she asked, her heart pounding at his nearness.

He chuckled. "Yeah, my grandparents used to have one. But not nearly as..." He paused, searching for the word. "Decorated like this."

A smile tugged at his lips as his eyes landed on the terrarium. "What's in here?"

He slowly moved past her, brushing her shoulder as he crouched in front of the tank.

She stepped back, watching him. When was the last time she had someone in her trailer? She thought for a minute that the vendor with the strange items booth was back in Nevada. Or it could be the guy from the bar in Wisconsin.

"That's Bambi. My rose-haired tarantula," she said, moving beside him.

"No shit," he answered in shock. "This is a fantastic setup. Does she travel well? Any issues with humidity in winter?"

"No, actually. It's probably the most well-built thing I own. Definitely sturdier than the bike." She laughed.

"Do you have any pets?" she asked. "Well, besides bees and... farm animals," she added with a little wave of her hand. She wasn't sure what exactly qualified as a farm animal.

His smile grew, lighting up his entire face. He looked over his shoulder at her.

"You're not going to believe this—"

Chapter Five

Lucas's face hurt from all the smiling.

Indie was remarkable. He'd thought he couldn't get her out of his head after the market, but now there was no way he could forget her.

The image of her joy and laughter when he'd admitted he also had a rose-haired tarantula replayed like a movie in his head. Compared to Bambi's beautifully curated terrarium, Randy lived in what Indie had dramatically called a "sleepy motel." She'd gashed a hand over her heart in mock horror, declared she was rescuing Randy from his tragic existence, and snatched Lucas's phone right out of his hand to plug in her number.

"Text me. Now," she'd said with a playful glare.

It had been a long time since anyone made Lucas laugh like that.

He felt lighthearted as he pulled into his gravel driveway just as his phone pinged.

He pulled it from his pocket. Indie.

His heart thudded as he opened the message.

All bandaged and clean.

Attached was a picture of her knees, rainbow Band-Aids bright against her skin, with a bar of soap sitting on her thighs.

He inhaled sharply, heat washing over him. His hand ached to trail along her thighs, the desire that had sparked when their skin brushed earlier now burning hotter.

He climbed out of the truck and headed for the front door of his small two-bedroom cabin, nestled at the edge of the family farm.

Before he could turn the knob, another ping.

Also, a terrarium picture. Now.

I mean, if you made it home.

I assume you didn't have to go far. You can get anywhere here in a few short minutes.

He smiled quickly, heading inside to fill her request.

The light from the window illuminated the tank in the corner. He crossed the room with purpose, heart lighter than it had been in months.

NICOLE LINETTE

Soul Creatures & Misunderstandings

NICOLE LINETTE

Chapter Six

Indie

Indie stayed up far too late putting together a box of items to spruce up Randy's terrarium. Lucas was right; the poor guy's tank was bland. Her body hummed slightly with the thought of seeing Lucas again. At the very least, this could be a gesture of thanks for helping her out yesterday. She looked down at her knees, remembering the brush of Lucas's hand against her. She hummed with pleasure. Reaching for her phone, glancing at her messages with Lucas, they spent the whole evening texting, and she had never felt so elated.

So… how's Bambi enjoying her bachelorette pad tonight?

She is amazing, but Randy is probably sulking. I think he wants to throw pillows and candles.

I don't think tarantulas use pillows.

That's because no one's ever offered. Revolutionary spider design is happening here.

Poor guy. Never knew he was missing out. He probably needs an interior decorator.

You were the one who called his terrarium "sad."

I said minimalist.

You meant sad. Admit it.

…Okay, maybe a little sad.

HA. Victory is mine. Randy shall live like royalty.

Should I be worried you're this passionate about arachnid decor?

You'll learn quickly, farmer man. I'm passionate about a lot of things.

...dangerous words.

Dangerous? Or intriguing?

Depends. Do you usually stay up past midnight talking about spider furniture?

Only with men who fix my bike chains.

Guess I'll take that as a compliment.

You should. It's rare.

Then I'll hold onto it, along with the mental image of Randy reclining on a velvet chaise lounge.

Omg yes. With a tiny crown.

...you're trouble.

The fun kind.

She smiled, stretching out. She could probably figure out where he lived and drop the supplies off on his porch. *What a great surprise,* she thought.

It didn't take long for Indie to track down where Lucas lived; one quick text to Sloane, and her plan was in motion. By noon, Indie was riding her bike with the new chain down the dirt road towards Lucas's. When Indie got closer to his house, she stopped and tucked herself behind a tree, peering around. She saw Lucas standing outside his door with a small woman whose blonde curls bounced as she walked. She couldn't make out what they were saying, but her feet felt frozen to the ground. The woman leaned in and hugged Lucas just as a little girl, about 5 years old, came running out of the house with her arms in the air. Lucas let go of the woman and scooped the little girl up and swung her around before cradling her and laying a kiss on her forehead. The girl squealed with delight as Lucas set her down. He waved as the woman and little girl climbed into their SUV and pulled out of the driveway.

Like he could sense her presence, Indie's phone vibrated in her pocket. She pulled it out, seeing a message from Lucas.

I have some free time this afternoon, would you maybe want to grab a late lunch?

Was he asking her out? The crunch of gravel mimicked the breaking of her heart. He was definitely married with a child, so why was he texting her? Anger boiled inside her. She thought he was a kind soul; his presence felt safe. How could she be so wrong? Any man who could flirt or step out on his wife was scum. She shoved her phone back in her pocket, watching Lucas head back inside before she got on her bike, fighting back tears as she rode her back to her van.

As Indie flung herself on the bed, the feeling of loneliness and abandonment that she kept buried deep down started to surface. She didn't like to be angry; she was a happy person who didn't let things affect her. However, this man, whom she barely knew, was turning her all topsy-turvy. She pressed her face into the pillow, letting the tears fall. This is why she never formed genuine connections with people; they either exploited her or abandoned her. Her body started to shake with sobs, and her phone continued to ping in her pocket.

Indie startled awake, not realizing she had fallen asleep. She could already tell her eyes were puffy from crying. She pulled her phone from her pocket; she had unread messages from Lucas, which she ignored, couldn't quite bring herself to erase, and some from Sloane. She opened Sloane's message and saw a gif of drink glasses clinking under it.

Girrrrrl I need a drink.

I was at a client's house, and this old guy came walking in. It's a better story in person.

Drinks tonight, plzzzzz

Indie cracked a small smile. She briefly thought about asking Sloane about Lucas, but doubt about admitting her curiosity crept in so instead she responded simply.

Yes, me too, when and where.

Tonight, she thought she'd put on her cocktail dress. She thought about Sloane's grocery store outfit. She was pretty sure she still had the dress for a party in LA, which she had attended with Clayton, the barista. It wasn't the most pleasant time, but it was a new experience, so she had chalked it up to a win. She would be in much better company this time, she thought.

Indie pulled up to the bar and stepped out, smoothing down her green cocktail dress and running her hands over her hair, catching any flyaways. She made sure to lock the van's door and even double-checked it by tugging at each handle. If she was so wrong about Lucas's character, maybe she was also wrong about this town, and she was not about to have anything stolen from her. She gave her head a shake. She did not like this version of herself, the skeptical version.

"This will be amazing, this will be fun, you are free, and nothing keeps you where you don't want to be. You make your own route and are in control of your own map," she whispered to herself, giving her the burst of courage and settling her back into the tranquil, playful space she lived in.

Sloane was already in a booth inside and jumped to her feet with a big wave when Indie walked in. "Girl, you look amazing! You look like a city girl ready to party the night away," she called, bringing Indie into a hug when she got close. Indie felt a little uneasy by the comment; she didn't want to stand out. She figured this was an appropriate outfit, but now she regretted it. As if Sloane could sense her hesitation, she released Indie from her hug, putting her hands on her shoulders and holding her at arm's length. "Hey now, don't you ever let anyone, especially me, make you feel bad for how you look. You are beautiful and have every right to wear whatever makes you feel like the goddess you are." Sloane grabbed her hand and pulled her into the booth. "Now let's get some drinks, the guava margaritas are fantastic."

Chapter Seven

Lucas

Lucas glanced down at his phone again. He wasn't sure what he said to cause radio silence from her, but it left a hollow pit in his stomach. He wasn't used to putting himself out there, and now that he had, she was ghosting him. Ghosting, he's pretty sure that's what the term was, but this felt more like she stole a piece of him and ran off into oblivion. *It should be called thieving,* he mumbled to himself. He took a seat on the couch. He never even took this girl out on a date, so why was he so shaken up about her ignoring him? A sense of resolve washed over him. Fine if she didn't want to go on a date or interact with him, he was sure someone else would. He pulled out his phone, fighting the urge to open the message thread to Indie, and scrolled down to the message chain.

> Hey, I unexpectedly have some free time this evening. Want to grab a drink?

Lucas walked into the bar, spotting Lauren in his regular seat. "Hey, man," Lucas called, approached, and took a seat. Lauren flashed him a knowing smile.

"You are either having work, family, or girl problems." Lauren laughed, patting him on the back and waving to the bartender. Lucas frowned, making Lauren laugh louder. "Man, you only ever want to meet me at the bar when you have a problem you can't do anything about." The bartender set down two more beers. "So which is it?"

"Woman problems," Lucas mumbled, grabbing one of the beers. "I don't know what I did, but I think I made her mad; she's not responding to me."

"Is it like the time you took a girl home and the goat attacked her?" Lauren asked with a smirk. "'Cause that was pretty funny, I could use another one of those incidents."

"You weren't even there," Lucas commented with a straight face.

"No, but we all felt like we were; slap heard around the world," an eavesdropper shouted. Lucas looked down the bar, spotting the owner of the grocery store. The people around him started to laugh.

"Small town problems," Lauren replied, smacking Lucas's back. "Now, who's the girl? Is it that new girl, Indie?" Lucas nodded. "Oh, she's a looker, actually, I think she might be here with Sloane." Lucas swore his friend's eyes turned heart shape at the mention of Sloane, but the thought quickly passed as he scanned the small room, spotting them at the back table.

"Maybe I should go over there." He moved to stand, but Lauren pushed his shoulder down.

"Not at all, looks like girls' night, you do not want to get mixed up in that, trust me."

"Yeah, or you'll get beer spilled on you," the man next to Lauren chucked, wiping his face with a cloth. The bar top customers busted out laughing.

Lucas decided it was best to give Indie space, but he sent them over a drink, which seemed to cause a chain reaction. Suddenly, others were sending them drinks and gawking in aah, and the two girls' laughter grew, and energy radiated over the bar. Lucas couldn't help but keep an eye on them, growing anxious about their ability to navigate safety. When the girls stood up to leave, he slapped some bills down; before Lucas could rise, Lauren caught his arm.

"For real, though, I know her type; they roll in and out of town. She's just looking to sleep with you, and then she'll be gone." Lauren frowned at him. "Don't get too attached, just have sex, let both of you get whatever this is, out of your systems."

"She isn't like that," Lucas responded, shoving up from his seat. His chest pounding, he hoped she just didn't want sex, because every inch of his body and soul screamed for her; it couldn't just be lust.

Lucas got in his truck and stayed far enough back to not startle them; his windows were down, letting their laughter and words fill his ears. He felt a little uneasy following them, but he just wanted to make sure they made it to Sloane's. He was unbelievably thankful they didn't try to drive.

Chapter Eight

It didn't take long for both women to down their first drink and then another. At some point, other patrons of the bar were smiling at them, laughing, and setting additional drinks at their table. It was as if they had their own show and everyone else was the audience. "He did not!" Indie laughed, patting the hand of an older woman who had come over to show off the dried flower brooch she had purchased from Indie previously.

"He did!" Sloane shouted. "This old man walked in on our yoga session and said, 'I'm definitely not going to need any Viagra today!'" They both started laughing again. It was remarkable how, even with interruptions, Sloane flawlessly carried out her story. Indie felt light, as if she hadn't spent the afternoon crying.

"Oh, look, it's Char! Hey, Char." Sloane jumped from the seat, bumping the table, sloshing the pitcher of, well, some booze. Indie was no longer sure what they were drinking. Sloane waved frantically at someone across the bar. Indie turned, and her heart dropped into her gut. The woman she had seen with Lucas strolled over, and Indie suddenly focused on Char's black skirt swaying around her slender legs and the clicking of her heels on the bar floor. She slowly looked up at Char's face. Indie could feel embarrassment washing over her; she felt like a little girl looking up at this woman. She could not fathom how any man would ever even look at someone else if they could spend their days staring at Char.

"Sloane, I told you I go by Charlotte now." Charlotte smiled, stopping at their table and giving Sloane a pat on the head. "Hi, I'm Charlotte," she said, holding out her hand to Indie. "I have heard such amazing things about your stand. I am really hoping to come by next time you set up. It's so nice to have something new in this town. My friend swears by your soap." Charlotte's pure innocence was radiating off of her, almost as if Indie could see flowers blooming in her wake.

"Um, hi," she whispered, clearing her throat and standing. "Hi, I'm Indie," she said louder, pulling herself together and taking Charlotte's hand. "I'm so glad you're hearing great things about my soaps. I'm sure I have a sample in my purse." She smiled, falling back into her bubbly personality, her safe zone.

"Oh, that is just wonderful." She clapped her hands. "Hold on, let me wave my husband over." She turned, waving a hand in the air.

Indie focused on her purse, her hands trembling with the thought of Lucas approaching. She took a deep breath, trying to level herself. She will pretend she did not know Lucas.

Slowly turning back to Charlotte, soap sample in hand, Indie gazed up at a tall man with brown hair and brown eyes. She instantly noticed his too-crisp shirt, with rolled-up sleeves that showed off his Rolex watch. He looked like a walking Wall Street ad, and he knew it. This was definitely not Lucas.

Her mouth dropped open in surprise. She snapped it shut quickly, but not quickly enough, as Charlotte looked between her husband and her suspiciously.

"This is my husband, Daniel. Have you met him already?" she said, raising her eyebrow.

"No, no, I just thought at first glance he was someone I knew from LA." The lie rolled off her tongue.

"I told you I looked out of your league," Daniel said in a tone that was too serious for Indie's liking.

"Well, it's hard to be in league with a goddess," Sloane said, blowing Charlotte a kiss. Indie held the soap sample out, a wave of relief washing over her, and then sudden panic struck her for ignoring Lucas all day. Did she blow her chance with him? Wait, did she want a chance with him? What did she want anyway? The alcohol must be getting to her.

Indie and Sloane walked arm in arm, giggling and swaying. "I can't believe," hiccup, "you thought Char was married to Lucas! They look so similar." Sloane laughed, tilting her head toward the night sky.

Indie blushed. "I thought it was just some weird small-town thing, like you all had some very distant relative."

"Gross, eww, eww, why would you put that in my mind?" Sloane responded, stumbling forward. Indie steadied them the best she could while the ground was wobbling. Indie wasn't quite sure how much they drank; she definitely never remembered feeling like this before. It was like an easy giddy feeling that wobbled between being dizzy and feeling floaty. "Girrrl..." Sloane slurred, dragging out the "r" sound. "I think I got us drunk," she said for the 10th time in their short walk.

"Yeah, I think so," Indie laughed, "I don't think I have ever been drunk before." She was smiling. Lucas was single; she had a new friend and was gaining a new experience. Indie loved new experiences. Indie's mind started to drift on other new experiences she could have in this little town when, suddenly, the jerk of Sloane's arm made her realize that Sloane had stopped moving.

"Oh my God," Sloane whispered loudly, the kind of whisper that's basically just yelling with slightly less air.

Indie froze, immediately alert. "What? What is it?" She spun around, looking for danger.

Sloane pointed dramatically down a grimy alleyway, where a mangy white and grey cat was aggressively digging in a pile of trash. "I think that cat is my soul pet."

Indie choked on absolutely nothing. "That? That's your soul cat?" She squinted. "You sure?"

"I can feel it with every piece of my being," Sloane said, making unblinking eye contact. "I need that cat." Her tone was the verbal equivalent of slamming a gavel.

Indie sighed. "Well, I guess we're catching a garbage goblin. Hold my earrings."

She untied the shawl from her waist with the precision of someone about to lasso a barn animal. Sloane followed her like an excited raccoon, trying and failing to muffle a giggle-snort.

"You aren't even wearing earrings."

"Was I wearing them when I arrived at the bar?" She reached up, touching her empty lobes. Sloane covered her mouth, trying not to laugh.

The cat, clearly sensing chaos, paused mid-rummage through the trash. It turned, arched its back, and hissed with the elegance of a deflating accordion.

"Shhh, baby," Sloane cooed, pulling out a bag of soggy takeout fries from her purse. "Good thing we forgot to eat these."

She tossed a fry toward the feline. The cat recoiled, then crept forward, curiosity warring with its streetwise instincts.

"We'll see how lucky we are having not eaten those when we're hungover and crying into a pillow tomorrow," Indie muttered as she crouched closer, her shawl poised like a net.

Sloane locked eyes with the cat. "Come to Mama, trash prince."

The alley held its breath. Somewhere in the distance, a dog barked. An owl judged them.

And the soul-cat sniffed a fry then, without warning, and bolted behind a dumpster.

"NO!" Sloane cried, lunging forward like she was trying to catch a train that had already left emotionally and physically.

Indie grabbed the back of her shirt just in time to stop her from face-planting directly into a suspicious puddle. "Easy, tiger." She laughed, hiccupping.

"But I felt it! It looked into my soul!" Sloane insisted, frantically digging in her purse for more fried ammunition. "I can still save this relationship."

"You've known him for twelve seconds, and he's already ghosted you behind a dumpster," Indie said, adjusting her shawl like a seasoned cat wrangler. "This is Tinder but with more fleas."

Another fry was lobbed. This time, the cat peeked out from behind the dumpster, one eye squinting suspiciously.

"Okay," Indie whispered, crouching again. "New plan. You circle to the left. I go right. If we can corner him—"

Sloane was already moving. "Got it. Like sheep dogs."

"Um... Exactly," Indie said. "Well, I assume, I have never actually met a sheep dog."

"Girl," Sloane said in her unique way that was starting to grow on Indie. "I think Lucas's farm has sheep dogs." She paused. "Wait, is it still a sheep dog if they don't have sheep?" Both women let out a laugh, and the cat raised its head instantly silencing them. "Come on, we need to get my soul cat," Sloane whispered.

They crept forward, slow and synchronized. As they closed in, the cat glanced between them, clearly calculating. It stepped forward to grab another fry, and Indie lunged.

Shawl out. Hands wide. A warrior cry that came out more like a panicked hiccup.

She missed. Sloane almost fell over laughing, but caught herself on a trash can.

The cat exploded into motion, leaping over Indie's back, bouncing off a trash can lid like a trampoline, and landing squarely on Sloane's shoulder like a parrot.

"AHHH!" Sloane screamed, spinning in circles. "It's ON ME. IT LOVES ME. IT HAS CLAWS."

"He chose you!" Indie shrieked joyfully. "He chose you!" Indie quickly tossed the shawl over the cat and pulled it from Sloane's shoulder. She could have sworn she heard ripping sounds as it detached from her dress. It hissed and spat but quickly seemed to surrender to its captors.

They both stood there, breathing heavily, hair askew, and the fry bag empty.

"I told you he was special," Sloane said, beaming. "It's already giving input on my outfit, the straps on this dress are terrible."

Indie stared at her. "You know, I think you're right, those straps are terrible..." she paused, "and this is most definitely your soul cat." She looked down into the little monster's eyes and could have sworn that it winked.

"Exactly. We're spiritually connected; however, I think now, I need a tetanus shot and another margarita." Sloane linked her arms with Indie. They both started to laugh, and Indie almost lost her grip on the cat. "Now what?" Sloane asked as they continued to her house, Indie keeping a firm grasp on the cat. "I have literally never owned a pet before." Indie let out a groan, and her smile reached her eyes. It was going to be a long night.

The long night didn't quite summarize the events that took place once they arrived at Sloane's home. As Sloane struggled to get the key in the lock, Indie tried to take in the details of the quaint white cottage. She didn't picture Sloane as the flower-growing type, but she had flowerpots hanging from the deck rail. The porch light gave everything a yellow tint. She peered around the corner of the house and could see a white picket fence. "I got it," Sloane cheered, drowning out the growls of the cat wrapped in Indie's arms.

In the drunken stupor, they decided to try to bathe the cat while Sloane called out different names, convincing Indie they would know when they said the right name. Indie was pretty sure Sloane was only saying the same couple of names on re-peat, but things were starting to blur together. They managed to pin the cat in the kitchen sink and give it a chaotic bath.

It ended with the cat streaking through the house, leaving a trail of water, and both women covered in clumps of hair and scratches. Their dresses were soaked and covered in pimple holes. Both girls glowed with accomplishment, though.

"At least it won't be leaving mud marks in my house." Sloane laughed, sliding down the kitchen counter to sit on the floor, a new beer somehow magically appearing in her hand.

"I think we need new clothes." Indie laughed, pulling a chunk of fur from Sloane's dress.

"Oh, I think we should text Lucas, he could bring us snacks!" she squealed, leaning her head on Indie.

"What?! He would not do that; he doesn't even know me."

"He would definitely bring you all the snacks. Which means I get snacks." She paused, and Indie thought maybe she'd fallen asleep. "I think I'm a snack whore." The two busted out laughing again.

"Okay, okay, but I can not be in this." She looked down at her outfit in the commotion, the dress had ridden up, exposing part of her ass.

"To the salon!" Sloane chirped, stumbling to her feet, and grabbing Indie towards her bedroom. Both girls screamed when they entered the room, and the cat jumped off the dresser in front of them before bolting from the room. "All relationships need work," Sloane deadpanned.

NICOLE LINETTE

Chapter Nine

Lucas

Lucas had just pulled on a pair of sweatpants and started his kettle for tea when his phone pinged. Excitement jumped in his body as he reached for the phone on the counter.

> I tried to ghost you, although aren't ghost souls that died then stay around to haunt people? It was probably more like I was trying to ignore you indefinitely. Anyhow, Sloane's here, you know her, she knows you. She said we need snacks, and I needed to respond to you because you aren't actually married.

> We might need tetanus shots. We found a cat.

> I think we are drunk.

The texts came one right after the other.

Lucas smiled down at the messages and hummed with joy when his phone notified him Indie was sharing her location; he couldn't help but hope she would share it indefinitely. Suddenly, the phone began to ring, and he answered it quickly. "Hey!" a drunk Sloane shouted into the phone. "We need snacks so much, like the most. Also, Indie thinks you're cute! She looked at your butt."

"Sloane, no," Indie's voice sounded through the phone, then there was a tussling sound and laughter.

"Sorry, she's drunk, we're drunk, but snacks are good. Can you bring snacks?"

Lucas took a deep breath, calming his speeding heart. "I will always bring snacks," he responded, turning off the kettle and leaving his tea unbrewed.

"Okay, thanks, bye." Indie sounded rushed before she hung up her shout, "No, don't feed cake to cats." Lucas's chest rumbled with laughter. He was often the designated driver for his sister, and that had led to some interesting adventures, but snack bringing, he sort of liked that.

Lucas was so grateful for Olivia's demand that they keep a secret snack bin in his house for her visits. He emptied the snack bin into a bag and returned to his truck; the engine hadn't even cooled. He didn't even need to follow the map to her location; he knew exactly where they had ended up.

Lucas knocked, but when no one responded, he tried the door, and it opened easily. He frowned, looking at the knob. A silver key glistened in the lock. He rolled his eyes, taking the key as he walked in. "Hey," he called out, hearing a scuttle from the back room. "Indie? Sloane?" He set the bag on the counter and walked towards the room.

Indie popped out of the back room. She wore blue shorts with a matching sleep top. "Shh, I just got her down," Indie responded with a slur, slightly swaying. Lucas peeked around the doorway, and Sloane was sprawled out on her bed, with a grey and white pile of scruffy fur next to her. "That's her soul cat," Indie whispered. "We fed it fries and chicken."

"It looks like it's gone through 7 of its 9 lives," he responded, squinting into the dark. "Is it missing part of an ear?"

"Yeah, and it has bald patches." Indie chuckled, taking a step forward, swaying more. Lucas threw out his arms to catch her.

"Seems like you had a great night, let's get you home."

"What about the snack?" Indie groaned. "I've never been so wasted, Bambi is going to be so disappointed in me." That was a surprise to Lucas; he figured she must have had a few party nights, people buying her booze and playing her favorite songs. "Oh, don't look so surprised." She batted at his chest with one hand. "Alcohol is nasty." She stuck her tongue out. Lucas guided them towards the door, grabbing the snack bag along the way.

"It's only nasty if you don't know what you're ordering," he commented, supporting her weight as she stumbled out the door and to the truck. Indie's eyes drooped. "Aaah, stay awake, we got to get some food and water for you, or tomorrow is going to suck." Indie let out another groan, and he swore he felt it reverberate in his core. He opened the truck for her.

"How does anyone even climb into your truck? It's so big," she groaned. He stifled a laugh.

"I'll help you," he said, setting the bag down, then gripped her hips, his thumbs grazing just under the bottom hem of her shirt. He looked down at her, his breath caught in his throat. He couldn't help but drop his gaze to her lips and let his thumbs ever so slightly against her skin. She sucked in her lower lip, and he felt like he was going to die. "Ready?" He managed to choke out, breaking their gaze. She nodded, and Lucas lifted her into the truck.

The ride back to Indie's camper was quiet; his thumbs tingled where they made contact with her skin. She sat quietly, drinking the water he brought and eating crackers. The quiet was strained more like electrification; every inch of him screamed to have slid his hand further up her shirt, to shove her against the truck, to let his mouth explore her. He cleared his throat to break the illusion.

"I'll help you get inside," he said, parked the truck, jumped out, and moved to her side. He opened her door and held out a hand. She took it with a shy smile and steadily stepped down from the truck. He followed her to the camper and ducked to go inside, his hand resting lightly on her back, arms ready to catch her.

"Well, here it is," she said, sitting down on her bed, causing the pastel yellow and orange comforter to flutter. He stepped back, worried at what he might do if he drew too close.

"There it is." He nodded.

"I should probably sleep."

"Yeah, that's probably a good idea." He continued to nod, she raised an eyebrow before letting out a sigh. Indie scooted back and wiggled herself under the blankets.

"Thanks for rescuing us," she mumbled, rolling on her side to look at him.

"I just drove you home, there was no rescuing." He stepped close and sat barely on the end of the bed.

"I wasn't drunk enough to not notice you making sure we made it to Sloane's. I don't know why you didn't help us with the cat." She let out a yawn, her eyes drifting closed.

"When you stepped down that alley, the last thing I expected was for you to catch a cat. I thought you had to pee, then you started shouting about cats." He shrugged, brushing her hair back from her forehead.

"When you find a soul creature, you have to catch it," she barely whispered, her breath becoming steady. He smiled down at her, thinking, *Yes, yes, you do.* He stood up, but before leaving, he removed her small butterfly earring from his pocket and set them next to Bambi's tank. He looked inside.

"Don't worry, I will always get her home safe," he whispered to the tarantula before heading back to his truck.

Ring Around the Wildflowers

NICOLE LINETTE

Chapter Ten

Indie

Indie's stomach turned, and her head pounded when she sat up in bed. She wasn't in her own pajamas, and the night came rushing back to her in hazy, glittering pieces. For a moment, the giddy sense of the evening seemed to temporarily wash away the hangover's fog and embarrassment that Lucas saw her wasted, until her stomach lurched again. She bolted from bed, bare feet slapping against the floor, and made it to the toilet just in time.

She groaned, wiped her mouth with toilet paper, and reached for her water bottle to rinse her mouth. Everything in her wanted fresh air and the slow sway of her hammock. She grabbed her phone, sunglasses, and a blanket before stepping outside.

The moment she threw the door open, the sun greeted her with warm waves of heat wrapping around her, while the sea breeze refreshed her. She blinked a couple of times, adjusting to the light, and then spotted a box sitting on her picnic table.

Excitement prickled along her arms. She loved surprises, especially pleasant ones. She opened the box, and sitting on top was a notecard, underneath was a hot-to-go cup, a pastry bag, and Advil.

She lifted the card and read:

> Thought this might help you out this morning. I hope you might let me take you out.

It was signed by Lucas.

His script was blocky, each letter pressed so firmly into the card that it almost dented the paper like he'd wanted to brand his words into it. Embarrassment washed over her with the realization of her drunken interactions with Lucas.

She lifted the cup and inhaled. Peppermint tea with honey filled her nose. She cradled the warmth between her palms. She took several deep breaths releasing the embarrassed feelings. She grabbed the pastry bag and retreated to her hammock, climbing in and snuggling with her blanket and the hot tea.

She opened the bag, and the smell of lemon poppy-seed muffins greeted her. She let out a happy sigh, breaking one apart and taking a slow bite. With each sip of tea and each swing of the hammock, her body seemed to purge the toxins she'd dumped into it the night before.

Her mind drifted uninvited but not unwelcome to the feeling of Lucas's thumbs brushing against her midsection last night. She imagined wrapping her legs around his waist, pressing her body against him, losing herself in the steadiness he carried. She could feel herself smiling into her tea.

Indie got her phone out, seeing a missed message from Sloane. She opened it first; it was a selfie of her in bed with the cat curled up on her pillow.

He loves me.

Yes, yes, he does, Indie thought with a smile before scrolling to the message chain with Lucas:

Good morning. I left you some sustenance on the table. Please reach out if you need any support.

Formal. But still endearing. Indie clutched the phone to her chest for a beat, letting the words settle in her chest before responding.

> Thank you for the treat! I love peppermint tea. Is this your family's honey in it?

The reply came almost instantly.

> Yes, it is.

A picture followed a jar of amber honey, catching the morning light.

Indie took a deep breath and typed one more message before she could overthink it:

> Let me take you on a date. 6 p.m.?

Chapter Eleven

Lucas woke feeling refreshed, images of Indie danced in his mind all morning as he tended the goats and bees. He had gotten up earlier to run some pastries and tea over to Indie. He felt overwhelming joy at his family's decision to hire farmhands a couple of years ago. It was hard to let go of the control of farming the land himself, but suddenly, he found himself thinking of other ways to fill his time.

The goat he was milking let out a bleating maa.

"Oops, sorry, Geraldine." He patted the goat's head and got back to milking.

He felt his phone buzzing in his pocket and fought the urge to check it. He's never been as distracted tending to his tasks as he was this morning.

Geraldine looked back at him and stomped her hooves. "Okay, okay, good girl, you're done." He unlatched her, and she jumped down, trotting on her way, but not before giving him one last side eye.

"She's always been the spicy one." Charlotte's voice sounded behind him. Lucas stood up, brushing his pants.

"I didn't think you'd remember, you haven't set foot in here in weeks," he responded, turning towards her, holding his arms out. Charlotte stepped in, returning the hug before tossing his hair.

"No real point since you've decided to take sole responsibility for them," she joked, following him as he covered the crate of goat milk and headed to the milk house.

"I feel like you're not just here to give me a hard time about milking goats," he groaned, holding the door open with his back for her to walk in.

"So perceptive, you are," she responded in her best Yoda voice, like she did when they were kids. "Actually, now that you mentioned it, can you handle the market in Blue Hill?" She gave him her charming smile and puppy dog eyes. He rolled his eyes.

"You know Olivia's puppy eyes are way more convincing." He threw a dirty rag at her. Charlotte caught the rag and tried to whip him with it, but he stumbled back, dodging and almost dropping his crate.

"Hey, now I have liquid gold here. You love Blue Hill, it was the one market you didn't want to give up when you begged me to take over this season."

He set the crate down to turn and give her his full attention. Her presence seemed to shrink; he saw her throat bob as she swallowed, as if she was fighting back tears.

"You know, I taught her those eyes," she croaked, regaining her composure. "Daniel and I were thinking it would be best if I didn't go out to Blue Hill this season. You know, just trying to figure out our family with Olivia going into kindergarten." She twisted her hair around her finger. Lucas felt the discomfort radiating off her.

"Well, I guess if that's what you want, but everyone is going to miss you. They know they can pull the wool over your eyes and get a better deal." He chuckled.

"That was one time!" she shouted, balling up the rag and throwing it at his face with a laugh. He let it smack him in the face.

"Oh, now you did it," Lucas said, trying to channel the free-flowing playful nature of Indie as he charged for his big sister, grabbing her up and tossing her over his shoulder. She squeaked in shock and kicked her feet, lightly pounding on his back.

"What are you doing!" She laughed.

"You'll see," Lucas responded, stomping towards the newly cleaned water trough. Charlotte glanced over and her eyes widened as she realized what he was planning.

"No, no, no, Lucas, don't you dare!" she screamed. Lucas started to swing her off his shoulder when a small laugh froze them. He turned to see Olivia's wide eyes staring at them.

"I want to play!" she squealed, running towards them and jumping in before either adult could respond. Lucas gave a shrug and plopped Charlotte into the water next to Olivia. Both girls started to laugh, and Olivia jumped on her mother, knocking her back and fully submerging her in the water. Lucas smiled down at what he used to think were the best two girls in his world, but now he felt like someone was missing, and maybe that someone was Indie.

Lucas stood watching mother and daughter splash around until Charlotte convinced him to get them towels. Then the two stood side by side watching Olivia run around the grass, the goat belting in the background either protesting the noise or the fact that they were not running with her. Charlotte had a towel wrapped around her shoulders.

"You know, you seem lighter today." She glanced up at him, mischief reflecting in her face. "I wonder if it has something to do with some purple van driving, totally opposite of you girl."

Lucas tried to smother his smile, failing to do so, he bumped her shoulder with his. He wanted to say, yes, and for some reason, you seem heavier, he felt like something was weighing his sister down.

Charlotte laughed, wobbling with the contact. "You remember when you brought that girl home in high school and introduced her to Geraldine the 1st?"

Lucas nodded, not sure where Charlotte was going.

"I swear all the dogs in Deer Isle were howling at her scream when Geraldine jumped on her. The mud splatter on her ass looked like she shit herself."

Charlotte laughed, earning her a glance from Olivia, who was crouched in the grass, probably looking for bugs.

"I don't remember it being so funny," Lucas grumbled, rubbing his face as he could still feel the sting of the slap he earned for laughing at the incident.

"After that, the girl would cross the street if she saw you coming." Charlotte leaned back on the fence, catching her breath with a deep inhale. "That's not even the worst incident of you bringing girls home."

She looked at him; he could feel his frown deepen, he was well aware of his luck with women he didn't need her to remind him.

"What I'm getting at is, I don't think Indie would mind mud on her clothes, or honey in her hair."

She shrugged, pushing off the fence and heading towards Olivia. "Come on, sweetheart, let's go check on Daddy."

Olivia let out a groan but ran to her mom and grasped her hand.

Lucas watched them go, imagining Indie exploring the farm. He could almost picture her lighting up when she stumbled upon the acres they left wild, as if his ancestors could sense a wild soul like Indie might need it. Like the universe knew his urge to speak with Indie, his phone chimed in the unique tone he set just for her. She sent a text.

> Thank you for the treat! I love peppermint tea. Is this your family's honey in it?

He quickly responded, finding a picture of the honey jar to send along with it. He started walking back to his truck when she replied.

> Let me take you on a date, 6 p.m.?

He stopped walking, unease creeping over him, not for the idea of going on the date with Indie but over the idea of not being the one to make and know the plans. Before his nerves of the unknown got the best of him, he responded.

NICOLE LINETTE

Chapter Twelve

Indie

Indie leaned against her van, feeling the warm sun against her skin. She spent most of the day in her hammock, nursing her hangover and texting with Sloane. Indie was pretty sure she would have to get Sloane a book on owning a cat, as all the text felt like questions about cat behavior and needs. Apparently, her soul cat decided her butterscotch candle was a snack and had taken a bite. Sloane had wrestled from its mouth, declaring she too loved butterscotch, but candles were not for eating. Sloane had since named the cat Butterscotch. Indie chuckled to herself, imagining Sloane wrestling wax from the cat.

"What's so funny?" Lucas's voice broke the silence. She opened her eyes, seeing him leaning against the bar wall, staring at her. She resisted the magnetic pull to walk to him and wrapped her arms around him.

"Just thinking of Sloane and her cat Butterscotch." Lucas raised his eyebrow.

"Oh." He pushed off the wall and stepped closer to her. She could see his chest rising and falling with each deep breath. She felt her breathing pick up to match his. "So what is the plan?" he growls, stopping inches from her, looking down. She felt like his breath was caressing her face.

"Flower picking," she whispered on a long exhale, meeting his eyes. He leaned forward, putting his hand on the van by her head. She felt her eyes fluttering as he leaned closer to her; she fought to keep his stare. He was so close that their foreheads were almost brushing.

"Sounds tranquil." He pushed back, breaking the trance. "Can I drive?" She nodded, unable to speak and holding out her van keys. "I meant my truck, but okay." He laughed, brushing her hand when he grasped the keys. Indie smiled.

It didn't take them long to find the field that Indie had previously driven by with wildflowers; it wasn't bountiful, but the flowers were perfect for picking and drying.

"So explain this to me again," Lucas said, parking the van. "You pick the flower, put them in essentially cat litter."

"I said like cat litter, it's not cat litter." She laughed, opening her door to get out.

"You put them in ESSENTIALLY cat litter, then make things."

"Yes, but I also sprinkle native seeds around, that's important, what we take we also give," she called from the back of the van, pulling a box out and two canisters. "Flowers go in the box, and then we run around and shake out seeds from these." She held them up, giving them a shake. She watched him take in the field and then her.

"You're going to wear that?" he asked with concern, pulling in his brows. She glanced down at herself. She was in her white dress with lemons and had abandoned her shoes on the drive.

"Yeah, this is what I normally wear." His eyebrows shot up in surprise.

"So you run barefoot, legs exposed in fields to create your crafts?"

"To create my living," she corrected and handed him a flower box and a shaker. "You should try it," she said, taking him in. He wore a button-up black shirt, blue jeans, and work boots. She blushed thinking of him running around shirtless and jeans rolled up, barefoot.

"Nope, nope, not happening. Wipe that smirk off your face," he responded as if he could read her mind. She set her box down and reached for his shirt, grasping one of the buttons between her thumb and forefinger. She could feel him stiffen under her touch; she dropped her hand with a laugh.

"First dinner," she declared, stepping back and picking up her box and the cooler bag that waited patiently in the back of the van. He reached out, taking the bag from her and also grabbing the blanket that was hanging out of the van.

"I'm interested to see what you packed," Lucas said, waving for her to lead the way.

Indie led them to a spot in the middle of the field. She could feel Lucas's eyes watching her closely, his protective nature sending threatening waves to any potential hazards in the area. She smiled, letting her steps grow more dance-like, adding a twirl to scoop down and clear the flower from the spot for the picnic blanket. She stepped back, looking at the space. Lucas laid out the blanket, and Indie fished the sandwiches and jars of sangria from the bag.

"So." Indie started sitting down and adjusting to move closer to Lucas after he sat. "You mentioned the family farm, so you grew up here? Have you ever lived anywhere else?" She handed him a sandwich and a jar. She stretched her legs out before folding them in, focusing on him. Lucas started to unwrap the sandwich.

"My family has owned the farm for six generations, and the house my parents are in has been passed down." He examined the sandwich. "Not that I live with them, I have my own cabin on the property, you can't even see their house," he responded quickly.

Indie nodded, feeling her cheeks blush again. "I haven't even been out of Maine, never felt the need to." He took a bite of his sandwich. Indie felt a lump in her stomach. "Where did you grow up?" he asked once he was done chewing.

"Sort of a hard question." She looked down at her sandwich. "I have visited a lot of amazing places all over the United States." She smiled, looking up at the cloudless sky. "I have been under this sky in hundreds of different places, and it's still just as amazing." She looked back at Lucas, who was staring at her.

"Even as a child? Don't children need structure or stability?" He seemed puzzled, like he was doing some challenging math problem.

"Oh no, I didn't really start traveling until I was eighteen. My mom loved the idea of traveling; she passed away when I was twelve, and I guess since then, my soul just wanted me to be free. I bounced around to a bunch of different foster families so that sort of developed my traveling skills." She recited the story easily; this was not the first nor could she imagine it being the last time she told it.

"Before I started traveling, I grew up in Astoria, Oregon."

"The Goonies is my favorite movie! I've always wanted to go to Astoria!" Lucas blurted out excitedly.

"I haven't. Been back to Oregon since I turned eighteen," she says at the same time.

They stared at each other for a long moment. Indie swore she could see a blush creeping up Lucas's neck.

"It's not a big deal, Astoria is beautiful, and I just decided to travel. There's so much world to explore, so much to see." She let her words trail off and quickly dismissed the thought of what it might be like to travel with another human, maybe this human?

Indie smiled quickly, allowing her energy to wash away the creeping curiosity that was growing on Lucas's face. "Come on, let's get to work." She waved her arms, indicating the wildflowers.

Indie allowed them to work quietly until their boxes were getting full. She could sense Lucas throwing her glances, like he wanted to say something or engage, but was too reserved or worried about disrupting her work.

Indie set her crate down on the blanket and stood tall, watching Lucas until he noticed. He smiled and said to her. "Did we get enough flowers?" he asked, setting his crate next to hers.

She looked at him with a smirk. "Have you ever, as an adult, run around without shoes or a shirt." *Or pants,* she added in her head, but felt like that was pushing it. He took a deep breath in.

"Not that I can think of." He looked at her, then around the quiet field. She could see the twitch in his fingers; he stood at the edge of freedom, only needing a spark of courage to step through.

Indie kneeled in front of him, pushing his pant legs up to expose his boot laces. She could feel the shudder that ran through his body as she slowly untied and loosened his boots. She tapped on his boot. "Lift," she commanded, lifting one foot. He nodded. She pulled the boot off, then the sock. She tapped the other and repeated the movement.

The air stood still as Indie rose in front of him. She placed her hands on his chest, maintaining eye contact until she undid the buttons, then she let herself glance at his chest.

This time she shivered seeing his chest and abdomen muscle, he had a small happy trail that trailed to the dip of his waistband. She cleared her throat, looking back up at him, and stepping back. "Come on, hand the shirt over." She held out her hand for his shirt.

He shrugged it off slowly and handed it to her. She tossed it on the ground, and she felt something snap in her when she looked at him standing there in only his jeans.

She let out a wild laugh and then took off running, calling out. "I bet you haven't even run as an adult!"

She run with her arms out like a child pretending to be a plane. The wind cooled her flushing skin and blew her hair behind her. She didn't look back, but she could hear his unsteady steps behind her.

She picked up her speed, screaming in glee.

Chapter Thirteen

His heart pounded seeing Indie kneeling before him. He couldn't move; he felt as if it would break this dream, and he would awake in bed alone. Time moved slowly, and he still wished for it to move more slowly.

She stood before him, unbuttoning his shirt, and he prayed that she couldn't see the bulge growing in his pants. He watched her studying him, and he thought he had never seen anyone so captivating, and he knew he would carve his own heart out for her had she asked.

He felt like the world around them stood still, then suddenly her eyes grew mischievous, she pressed her hands on his chest, and then pushed gently before turning and running, a wild sound exploding from her.

Something in him snapped; he wanted to be the one causing her to make those noises.

"I bet you haven't even run as an adult," she called, to which he took off after her.

She looked like a fairy, the wind tangling in her dress and trailing behind her like wings, her feet barely seeming to touch the ground as she ran.

She was right. He hadn't truly run in years. He chased Olivia around the yard or occasionally a goat or two, but this, this was different; it was exhilarating, it felt as if a piece of him that was locked away was suddenly released.

Indie seemed to slow her laughter, softening, and Lucas crashed into her. He wrapped his arms around her, turning to fall to the ground on his back, her head tucked against his chest. He was breathing heavily as he searched her face. Tears from the wind stained her rosy cheeks, and her smile seemed to brighten the darkening sky.

"Wasn't that amazing?" she asked, crossing her arms on his chest and resting her head on them. She seemed to be studying his face.

"You were right. This was a different type of running." He let the tension release from his hands, fanning his fingers out, taking in the feeling of her bare skin under his palms.

"I'm right quite often, according to Bambi." She laughed.

He could feel her heart pounding against his chest. He let his fingers draw circles on her shoulder blades. He watched the clouds moving above him as his breath started to return to a normal, steady pace.

And for a second, it felt like the whole world had conspired to give him this moment. Just him, and her, and the sky.

"What is it like living like this?" he asked, taking a deep breath.

"Live how?" she responded in a sleepy voice.

"Without responsibility, like a child running free." He thought of Olivia running around the yard and Indie running around the field. His heart ached to be able to be like them, but his brain kept him grounded.

It took him a minute to realize that at some point Indie had stiffened in his grasp.

"I think it's time to go," she whispered, pushing off his chest. He fought the urge to tighten his grasp and to keep her. A fleeting thought passed through him: you can't contain the wind.

He pulled the van up next to his truck. He got out of the van, hoping to make it to Indie's door before she opened it, but she moved quickly. He could feel his body stiffen with concern. Lucas wasn't sure what had happened. He felt like things were going well, but then it felt like a storm rolled over Indie and swept away her joyous mood.

Lucas held out his arms to her, giving in to the urge to comfort her, but he sensed hesitation. She stepped in, wrapping her arms around his waist and briefly laying her head on his chest. She pulled back quickly; it was like a soft blanket being brushed over briefly before it was stolen, leaving him unsatisfied.

"... did I do something wrong?" he says, stumbling on his words, obviously nervous.

"I have to go," she blurted out quickly moving to open her car door.

"Drive safe," he whispered, gulping down a knot. He had never had the urge to cry before, but suddenly he felt the pressure building in his chest.

Indie gave a small smile before nodding and climbing into her van. Lucas watched her drive away. There was no relief in thinking she was just a short drive away because every part of her presence screamed she was ready to fly away on the next gust of wind. Once she was out of view, he got in his truck to drive home, hoping he could solve the riddle that was Indie.

Mr. Bad Attitude

NICOLE LINETTE

Chapter Fourteen

Indie

Indie stirred with discontent, slowly waking. Her dreams for the first time in a while snuffed her energy, her joy. Memories of adults screaming at her for being childish, demanding more from her, until she couldn't even recognize herself. She was a robot trapped in a child's body.

They wanted the house clean, she cleaned it, they wanted her to cook, and she did, the babies needed tending, and she did that.

The robot of her became so entwined with the requirements of the adults that it started to transform her into one far too soon.

She remembered caring for newborns and toddlers at all hours of the night because if she didn't, they were left to cry and she couldn't bear the sound of their desperation. She would change them, rock them, sing them songs while trying to give them all of the love she used to get from her mom because she knows they have never felt that love before.

She remembered the pain of switching homes and knowing those babies won't be loved anymore.

It's midnight and she could hear Anna crying again. This is the third time she's been up with her since she put her to bed at 7:30. She had done Anna's normal nighttime routine: snack, bath, teeth brushed, reading books, and finally bedtime.

She didn't know what else to do, other than hold her and show her she is loved. She moved quietly into the room, scooping Anna up out of the old wooden crib. Indie made cooing sounds as she settled into the rocking chair.

"It's okay, baby, shh, my sweet girl." Slowly, as Anna drifted asleep in her arms, her eyes started to grow heavy as well.

Indie startled awake to her foster mom Lynn screaming at her.

She must have fallen asleep while rocking Anna back to sleep. It was hard to remember the slur of insults and demands Lynn hurled at her. The kids were up, breakfast wasn't done, the list seemed to drag on. Indie fought back the urge to explain, to advocate for herself, but she knew her words would fall on deaf ears. Anna stirred in Indie's arms, her little whimpers growing louder as Lynn continued to scold her.

"Yes, ma'am." Quickly, she got to her feet trying to display no emotions. Lynn stormed from the room and Indie got to work situating Anna so she could complete her other chores. As she worked, she thought about how lucky she was for every minute of love she received from her mother, and she hoped someday she and all these other children would receive that sort of love.

She let out a groan when her phone, sitting across the trailer, started to chime. The sound startled her as she typically didn't need an alarm, but she had a sixth sense that today she might have needed it. She climbed from the bed, stopping in front of Bambi.

"Hey girl, remind me to tell you about yesterday when I get home." She spotted her little friend making her way to her burrow. She grabbed her phone, seeing several missed messages from Lucas and Sloane, and one missed call from Eleanor, as if her oldest friend sensed that Indie needed her.

She inhaled and opened Sloane's messages first:

Butterscotch stole my dinner last night while I was in the bathroom.

I can't decide if I should have a bubble bath and read a book or watch my new TV show tonight.

Either your date is going super well, like you're tangled up all night (laughing face) or he's bored you to death.

Fine, I'll go to bed (Cry face). Come to yoga tomorrow morning Plz.

She looked at the clock; she had plenty of time to make it to yoga and prep for the market. She started her water kettle to make tea and opened Lucas's messages.

Hey… I am checking in to see if you are okay.

Thank you for the evening. I don't think I've ever had an experience like that.

Indie ignored Lucas's messages. He was just like everyone else; he saw her as a child, like one of Peterpan's lost boys, forever stuck in some land of make-believe. She wasn't, though; she spent years peeling away at her skin, painfully shedding, and growing. She growled, pouring the water into her cup, then responding to Sloane

Butterscotch is the cutest troublemaker. Are you still doing yoga this morning?

There was an instant response.

Yes, see you soon!

Indie spent the morning drinking her tea and setting up her supplies for the market. She removed the flowers from yesterday from the van and set them under the picnic table. She wasn't ready to do anything with them, afraid that they would send visible images of running through the field with Lucas. She also didn't want to toss them; it would be like denying some sense of grounding that had started to grow in her, almost like the buds of roots were starting to force their way out of her and into the ground here.

Chapter Fifteen

Lucas

Lucas spent the night tossing and turning. He knew he had done something wrong to cause Indie to yell at him, but he wasn't sure what. He took deep breaths, refocusing on the task at hand.

He made quick work of doing his farm chores and packing for the market. Getting in the work truck to head to the market, his phone pinged. He was startled, having forgotten that it existed. He looked at the screen.

Thanks again for doing this (Heart).

His chest felt heavy.

He sent a heart to Charlotte's message.

Time moved in a haze, and before he realized it, he was done setting up the stand. Others had just started arriving and tending to their spots.

He gave small smiles to the familiar faces, but his heart wasn't in the moment.

He just wanted Indie to respond to him, or to go to her and fix whatever he did.

Lucas stepped back, looking at his stand from the customer side, when a lavender van pulling in caught his eye. He felt his heart jump in anticipation of seeing Indie.

Chapter Sixteen

Indie

Indie strolled into the park wearing her practically new neon purple yoga pants, a matching sports bra, and a sky-blue zipped hoodie. The outfit was practically new, and the softness of the fabric helped to settle her.

Indie quickly picked Sloane out of the group of women standing among rolled-out yoga mats. She was chatting with women; every gaze seemed transfixed on her. Indie wondered if Sloane knew how powerful her presence was. Sloane spotted her approaching and waved to her to join.

Indie smiled, and warmth washed over her, and the group of women made space for her. Indie was amazed at how easily the women of Deer Isle seemed to make space for each other.

"Indie, I'm so glad you were able to join us," Sloane beamed, giving her a hug. "You are going to feel amazing after these next 45 minutes."

"Oh, most definitely," an older woman replied as the ladies began to gravitate towards their mats. "Sloane does wonders for the soul and body. I always feel my best after these mornings in the parks with her," several other women muttered and nodded in agreement.

"Well then let's get started." Sloane clapped with excitement, taking her place at the head of the class.

Indie inhaled. Her body and mind felt better after yoga and girl time with Sloane and other women from Deer Isle. She smiled to herself, climbing from the van and grabbing her items.

She smiled at the other vendors setting up as she headed to her spot. Some waved, and others nodded. She felt their eyes following her, so she kept her head high and her face welcoming. She continued to scan the rows until she spotted her spot and at the same time a very familiar figure, Lucas.

She turned fully towards him and held his gaze. His eyes seemed clouded with pain. She kept her composure and continued to her spot and made quick work setting up the whole time, feeling Lucas's stare boring into her from a couple of booths away.

It didn't take long for customers to arrive, and with their emergence, Indie couldn't fight the urge any longer to look out and check on Lucas. He was talking with a customer but looked at her as if he could sense her gaze, so that she could see his. Her phone pinged.

Hi.

She looked at the phone and started to debate whether she wanted to reply or not. A grumble broke her thought. A tall, frowning man in flannel and jeans, not too different from Lucas's own outfit, stood before her booth. The man wore a faded baseball cap that only allowed peaks of grey hair to poke through.

"Oh, sorry, I'm Indie, welcome to my stand, do you have any questions?"

"Ten dollars for dried weeds?" he barked, flicking one of her flower crowns. "Back in my day, girls your age didn't waste their time on frilly hobbies. We all had to learn real skills. Work worth paying for."

Indie tilted her head, smiling politely. The man continued, "And these," he gestured to the soap display, "you probably watched a couple of YouTube videos and decided you were a businesswoman. Bet your parents are still paying your rent, unlike the rest of us hard-working folks around here. You should just go home to your mommy, little girl."

Indie laughed lightly and leaned forward, picking up a rosemary-mint bar. "This one's good for stress relief. Might be perfect to help wash away your bad attitude and bring you more customers, as it seems you're so starved for them, you want to make others feel just as bad." Not once did Indy's voice rise or her face falter. She could hear some gasps and snickers coming from around her. The man opened his mouth, shut it, and shuffled off.

Indie sat back down in her chair, looking up and making direct eye contact with Lucas as he strolled over.

Chapter Seventeen

Lucas

Lucas didn't fight the urge to watch Indie any time he wasn't interacting with a customer; he was watching her. She moved gracefully around the booth, her smile drew customers in, and they all walked away with at least a sample.

"Lucas!" a familiar woman's voice drew his attention. "I didn't know you were coming this week. I was expecting Charlotte." The little grey-haired woman hunched over on a cane moved into his booth.

"Ms. Hummington," Lucas responded, coming around the table to grasp her hand.

"Oh, honey, how have you been? Enjoying more free time with the farm hands back to work?" She moved to straighten out his jars of honey.

He smiled softly. "It's definitely been a change." He glanced at Indie, and one of the other vendors was engaging her in interaction; the man looked stiff.

Ms. Hummington coughed. "You know that girl? She's cute." She gave him a knowing smile. Lucas stumbled over his words in surprise. He kept Indie in his sight while glancing at Ms. Hummington.

"Yeah, we have met a couple of times. She might be mad at me, I'm not sure," he found himself saying unintentionally.

"Did you ask her? If she was upset."

Lucas looked fully back over at Indie. "I guess I haven't," he said quietly. Indie seemed not to be enjoying her interactions. "Excuse me, Ms. Hummington, I'll be right back."

"Oh, take your time, honey," she responded, moving around the back of the booth and sitting in his seat.

Lucas took big steps, quickly closing the space between him and Indie. Suddenly, the man took a step back, seeming flustered. Indie sat in her chair, making eye contact with him. The man's face was red as he turned and walked away.

Lucas stopped across the table from Indie. "Are you okay?" he said, suddenly he felt unsure of what he was doing. He could feel Indie looking him over.

"I'm okay, it's not the first time a man has overlooked my abilities because they think I'm a child, and it won't be the last," she kept her tone light, but it threw daggers at him.

"What do you mean?" he asked, staring down at her, heart racing.

"People often think because of the way I live and how I present that I'm somehow less of an adult. They don't see the work and planning that goes into living the way I do." She kept eye contact with him. Lucas nodded along the alarming realization that he had also been one of those assholes; a wave of shame washed over him.

Lucas's expression softened as he met her gaze. "You're right," he said gently. "I'm sorry, I made an assumption. That wasn't fair to you." He paused, letting the weight of his words settle. "The way you present and live is new to me. I see the joy and love you manifest, and I chose a poor way to express how in awe I am of you." The words tumbled out; he was sure others stopped to listen, but he kept his focus on her. "You are brave, and I am jealous of the boundaries you have pushed. I have never left my home; I am the childish one." He closed his mouth, studying her face, hoping she knew he was reflecting the truth.

Indie let out a laugh. "I doubt anyone has ever described you as childish." She inhaled. "It's too tiring to be mad about things people don't understand."

She stood up. Walking around the table, he stood to meet her. He held out his arms, and she walked in. The sounds of awe filled his ear, and the beating of her heart against him filled his soul.

"I am sorry," he whispered, inhaling the scent of her. "Let me make it up to you. We are having a shore dinner tonight. Please join me."

"You want me to meet your family?"

"Well, you already met Charlotte and Daniel, and I don't want to give you a chance to change your mind if I put off the date for tomorrow. I don't think I can wait until tomorrow." Indie's laugh filled his ears, and every part of him felt right holding her, listening to her, like the last piece of his puzzle was finally found.

Oh Sh... Shore Dinner

NICOLE LINETTE

Chapter Eighteen

Indie has agreed to go to a family dinner at Lucas's. Her camper has clothes, shoes, and accessories tossed all over the place. She can tell she is feeling nervous because usually she is pretty simple and has no problem picking out an outfit. She has a strong need to pick the perfect outfit to impress his family, though.

She texted Sloane:

> I'm going to Lucas's family house for dinner, help me.

She included a picture of clothes thrown around her camper. Indie had been on plenty of dates before, but not typically second dates, or to a family house. Her phone rang. Sloane was video calling her.

"You are gonna be fine. His family is so chill. You met Char; she's the biggest sweetheart. Also, hold up the pink thing, is it a dress?"

Indie sets the phone against Bambi's tank. She grabbed the garment and held it up.

"Nope." Not that Sloane responded.

Indie looked at the screen, noticing Butterscotch lying across the top of the couch, his tail occasionally flicking Sloane's head. She smiled; they were a cute pair. The next twenty minutes were spent holding up garments and Sloane dismissing them.

Indie ended up settling on a simple white dress with a blue floral design. And a simple pair of stud earrings. She normally was more fun and colorful, but trying to play it safe. She sprayed herself with some of her favorite perfume that she has been using for years; it has notes of wild strawberries and jasmine.

Sloane's doorbell rang as the perfect outfit was chosen. She ran to the door, leaving Indie to stare through the phone at the empty couch. Sloane returned, holding up a bag of Chinese food.

"My friend, you look amazing, you are so beautiful. Tonight is going to go spectacularly," she said in a reassuring tone. Indie nodded, taking slow breaths.

"Thank you, Sloane. I hope your dinner is amazing as well." Indie smiled nervously. Sloane blew her a kiss.

"Go have fun and remember all the details to fill me in later." Sloane gave a little wave before blowing Indie a kiss and hanging up.

NICOLE LINETTE

Chapter Nineteen

Lucas

The kitchen smelled like home. Salt, butter, and the faint briny snap of clams steaming on the stove. My mother was already in her element, moving between the pots like a conductor, while Dad worked the grill outside, coaxing the lobster tails to perfection. Charlotte leaned against the counter, laughing at something Olivia said as she fumbled with an ear of corn, trying to pull the husk.

Lucas was excited to have Indie join them for shore dinner, but while he usually felt at ease, the nervousness was creeping into his stomach this time. Indie would be walking into the noisy warmth of the family's kitchen for the first time, and Lucas just wanted her to feel like she had a place here.

Lucas was hyperaware of every detail. The clatter of the pans. The warm chatter. The way Daniel was planted in the recliner in the other room, pretending not to hear Charlotte ask him twice to help set the table. He'd muttered something about not wanting to "get in the way" but kept the TV blaring just loud enough to make conversation harder. He caught his mom's jaw tightening, though she didn't say a word. This was their family thing, their tradition, and Daniel sitting it out was his way of making sure they all noticed.

"You are a mess!" Charlotte laughed, picking up the pot of corn to take outside to the grill. Lucas frowned, realizing she was talking to him.

"It's because he's bringing a girl into this chaos," Daniel called from his recliner. Lucas watched Charlotte's face as her smile faltered at Daniel's comment.

"Indie is going to love this. We are fun, our house is cute, and we have all the great food." She inhaled deeply, winking at him as she pushed the screen door open and called out for their father.

Lucas looked at his mother, who was trying to hide her smile.

"What is it?" he asked, moving to the stove and peering into the pot of clean oysters.

"Oh, it's just nice to see you having people over. We haven't even seen Lauren in months. I was worried you were becoming a human version of Randy." Lucas's mother initially hated the idea of the pet tarantula, but Randy seemed to be growing on his mother. Lucas gave a chuckle. "You must really like her."

"I think I do," Lucas responded, not expressing his concern that he was falling for a woman who was nomadic. Lucas headed to the front door to be outside to greet Indie.

"Food will be ready in 30," his mother called to him. Lucas had just made it to the porch when he spotted Indie's van coming up the gravel drive. She pulled up next to his truck. He felt like he was holding his breath as she exited the van, smoothing down her dress. Her hair was put up in a bun with flowers woven in. She gave him a smile, turning her back to him and reaching into the van to pull out a dried flower bouquet and a small bag. Heat washed over him as he studied her bare legs. He cleared his throat as she turned back to him.

"Hi," he said, stepping closer. "You look amazing." He glanced down at her body, feeling his temperature rise.

"Thank you." She smiled, closing the space and giving him a brief hug. "You look nervous, you don't have to be," she said, grabbing his hand, entwining their fingers. "If anything, I should be the nervous one, isn't that how it's supposed to be?"

He let out a chuckle. "Well, I haven't had the best experiences bringing prior dates home."

She stood on her toes and gave him a kiss on the cheek. "Oh it will be okay, who is all here?"

"Everyone's here," he responded, leading the way but keeping her hand in his.

As soon as he opened the door, he spotted Charlotte, Olivia, and his mother running and ducking back into the kitchen. He frowned. "Sorry, they are nosey." Indie just smiled and followed him in.

"This is Daniel, I think you met him and Charlotte at the bar." He gave Daniel a nod, while pulling her towards the kitchen.

"I think butterscotch gives off better vibes than he does," she whispered to him. Lucas smiled.

"This is my mom, Josephine." His mother was smiling and holding her hand out when they entered the kitchen. Indie took her hand, giving it a shake, and then handed her the flowers and bag.

"It's great to meet you, thank you for having me over for dinner."

"No, thank you for coming, it has been so long since we have had any new friends at dinner." She gave Lucas a wink. "I think the girls and Hank are outback. I set out some drinks and fruit. Please help yourself, and we'll have dinner here soon." Lucas nodded and gave an arm wave for Indie to head through the screen door.

Lucas could hear Olivia screaming with joy as she climbed up the plastic slide, Otis following right behind her.

"Does that goat only have three legs?" Indie asked, stepping out onto the porch. Lucas and Charlotte looked at them with a smile crossing Charlotte's face and a curious look crossing his dad's. Lucas had the sense he should have prepared Indie for his family.

"It does, that's Otis, he's a house goat, and the wild child over there is my daughter Olivia. Olivia, come say hello," Charlotte called. Olivia twirled around to face them, her excitement clear on her face.

"I've heard so much about you, I'd love to talk shop sometimes. You know my family has a long history of attending markets. Maybe we can give you some pointers." Hank stuck out his hand. Lucas frowned at his dad.

"I'm always up for learning," Indie responded, grasping the hand. "I've attended many different types of markets and showcases. I'm sure I can return the favor." Charlotte's eyes grew wide at Indies' remark. They all waited for Hank's response. He let out a deep laugh.

"I like you, Indie. Let me pull these off the grill and check on JJ." Hank was still laughing as he moved inside. Charlotte let out a breath similar to the one Lucas was holding.

"Lucas!" Olivia cried, crashing into his legs. He scooped her up. "Is that the lady who's pretty and new?" Lucas nodded.

"Indie, this is my niece, Olivia."

"Come here, Olivia, let's go get you washed up." Charlotte held out her arms for Olivia, who groaned in protest but ultimately went with her mother. "I'm glad you made it to dinner, Indie, it's been kind of boring here lately."

"Glad to be here," Indie responded. Lucas shifted his weight on his feet. He could feel the energy vibrating off Indie now that they stood alone.

"So you grew up in this house?" she asked, leaning against the rail and gazing up at the house.

"Yeah, we lived here with my grandparents, but both Charlotte and I built our own houses on the property a couple of years ago. I lived with Lauren for a while after high school. Lauren is a guy I grew up with," he added quickly, not wanting her to think he had lived with a woman. He didn't even want her to think he had ever been serious with someone else. He wondered if she had ever been serious with someone. He thought about another guy sharing her trailer, sharing her small bed. The thought made anger turn in his stomach.

"You okay there, big guy?" Indie whispered, setting her hand on his shoulder.

"Oh, sorry, I was just thinking." He smiled at her.

"About?" she asked, looking down at Otis, who had made his way to the deck. She reached down and gave him a scratch behind the ear.

"I don't think I've brought anyone home, like a date, since high school." He saw a smile across her face, and he felt like the world got brighter.

"I haven't brought anyone back to my trailer either," she whispered with a wink. Just then, the screen door flew open, and his mother stepped out.

"Food's on," she sang, setting the platter of seafood down, and the rest of the family followed, carrying the rest of the dishes.

"This smells amazing." Indie smiled, stepping back from him.

NICOLE LINETTE

Chapter Twenty

Indie was laughing so hard her face hurt. Lucas's family was hilarious. She didn't think his face could get more red after the first couple of stories, but then Charlotte shared a story about him finding a wild dog and bringing it home only for his mother to drop her pie while screaming for them to get out. The dog he found had actually been a skunk. Lucas spent the next two days sleeping outside in a tent until they could wash the stink from him.

Indie helped Lucas's mom finish up the dishes while Lucas cleaned the grill. "So Indie, tell me a little bit about yourself. Where are you from?"

Indie took a deep breath, taking a moment to reflect as she dried a plate. "I'm from Astoria, Oregon but have moved around a lot." She paused to allow Josephine to respond.

"Oh, I've heard Oregon is beautiful. I've lived here my entire life, my dad and I did some traveling when I was younger, but mostly stayed in the northeast. Hank isn't much to get out of his routine so we pretty much stay around here. I would love to hear more about your travels one day. I can live vicariously through you." Josephine let out an effortless, warm laugh, that caused Indie's smile to grow.

"So you and Hank grew up together?" she asked, watching Josephine carefully line the silverware up to dry.

"Oh yes, he swears we met at a park in preschool, but I don't think we met until kindergarten. He was the first person to call me JJ after another kid accidentally pronounced my name as Jose-a-pee." Josephine started to laugh again and this time Indie couldn't help but join in.

Indie was feeling light but in a different way than how she felt when she was hitching her trailer to go to her next destination. She couldn't remember ever having a real family dinner with stories, and laughter. Not to mention how the Carringtons seemed to fall into a sense of teamwork, serving and cleaning up dinner. She could see how all those traits allowed them to have a successful farm.

"Hey," Lucas called, walking into the kitchen, making eye contact with her. "If you're good in here, I was hoping to take Indie around the farm?"

His mom seemed to be giving him a mischievous smile. "Watch out for the goats." Lucas rolled his eyes, Indie raised her eyebrows at him. "And you should take the four-wheeler. It's a nice evening for a drive, helmets are on the shelf."

Lucas grabbed her hand, his warmth radiating into her fingers. "You want to take a four-wheeler ride with me?"

Indie beamed following him out. "I would love nothing more than to ride with you." Indie felt her face get hot and glanced at Lucas, his cheeks were pink. "I mean I'd like to ride the four-wheeler," she said quickly. Lucas laughed and led her to the side of the house.

Indie loved the four-wheeler and not just because she could feel Lucas pressed against her, allowing her to drive and point direction to guide them. She loved the wind on her skin and adrenaline coursing through her, the movements of the four-wheeler connected her to the ground in a way she'd never felt before. She was embarrassed that the whole situation made her insides heat, especially as Lucas pulled her tighter against him when she hit bigger bumps.

They stopped outside a picket fence area; the fence looked new, but the beehives on the other side appeared older, more worn. Lucas climbed off the four-wheeler and held a hand out to her.

"These are the bees, well, one hive system. We have another set on the other side of the farm, but these are the ones I'm in charge of," he replied, stopping next to the fence.

She studied the fence, noticing how sturdy and secure it looked, but also beautiful. The white pickets seemed to glow against the field, enhancing the colors of the flowers and drawing your eye to the beehive. She smiled at the sign hanging lopsided on the gate: "You shall not pass."

"What's up with the fence? It seems... different? Compared to the other fences I've seen?" Lucas laughed at her choice of words.

"The purpose is solely for Olivia; Charlotte was worried she would wander out there and stumble into the beehive. So maybe it won't keep everything out, but it will definitely keep a wild child out."

Indie blinked in disbelief. "You really think she'd make it all the way out here by herself?"

Lucas shrugged. "She is her mother's daughter, so I wouldn't put it past her. Come on, I'll drive." He led them back to the four-wheeler. Indie looked around at the wildflowers and bushes. This area was well-maintained; she could sense the work and the love Lucas put into it.

"Are you saying I'm not a good driver?" she joked, climbing on behind him and wrapping her arms around his waist. She felt his muscles tighten from her touch and had a feeling she was blushing again.

Lucas gave her the tour of the farm, stopping outside the goat barn. Lucas hesitated getting off the four-wheeler. "Just don't slap me," he said, slightly too serious for her liking.

"What?" Indie responded, confused, hopping off.

She was going to question him further, but suddenly goats poured out of the barn into the fenced pen. "Oh my god," she squealed, running up to the fence. She didn't expect so many shades of brown, creams, red tones, and patterns. She didn't have a lot of experience with creatures outside of Bambi, and well, the occasional cats and dogs. She stuck her hand through the fence, and a little goat tried to suckle her fingers.

"That is Screwdriver," Lucas replied, walking to the gate, unlocking it, and waving her over. "He's a little nutty." Indie entered the pen, and the goats swarmed them, belting and using their teeth to pull at her dress. She let out a loud laugh and gave them ear scratches while pulling her dress free from them.

"This is amazing." She crouched down, rubbing foreheads with one. She could feel Lucas watching her closely. Suddenly, the goat she was nuzzling jumped up. Putting their hooves on Indie's shoulders, but instead of crashing backwards, Indie steadied herself. "Wooh now, lady, I'm not quite ready to dance." She scratched the goat's hackles and pushed her off. Indie stood up, brushing her dress off. She turned to find Lucas looking worried.

"Oh, it's just a little dirt." She laughed, walking up and giving his shoulder a pat. "What goat was that?"

"Maggie," he responded, "she is a curious one." He followed her as she walked around the goat pen, petting the goats and cooing at them.

"Is that a garden over there?" Indie asked, pointing outside the pen. Lucas gave a nod.

"Yeah, nothing too crazy, I was bored. I have some tomatoes, strawberries, cucumbers, and some bell peppers." He shrugged. It wasn't anything impressive in his mind. Indie patted Maggie before exiting the pen.

Chapter Twenty-One

Lucas

Lucas felt like he was in a dream: the soft light of the evening sun dancing, the clink of silverware, and echoes of laughter. Indie moved effortlessly through this childhood home, her presence warming every inch of him. He felt as if the whole family was pulled into her orbit; it was easy and unforced, like she was meant to be there. He caught himself smiling just from her presence. As dinner was winding down, he wasn't ready to wake from this dream, and he had his arms wrapped around her waist as she drove the four-wheeler like she was trying to take flight.

"Well, let's take a look. I bet it's amazing." She walked with a sway like a dance move, and he followed behind, entranced. Indie walked quicker, and he briefly lost sight of her around the corner of the garden.

"Oh my god!" He heard her screech, and he flung himself forward in fear, just to find her standing smiling at him and holding a tomato with a bite taken out. "This is amazing." She laughed, giving him a wink as if she could hear his pounding heart. Lucas stepped closer to her so they were chest to chest. He looked down into her eyes, letting her feel his heart and panicked breath. Indies smile softened, and she let the tomato slide from her fingers like she forgot she was holding it. He would have made a joke about it, but her hands laced behind his neck, bringing his lips closer to her. He felt the energy pulsing from her lips onto his, and he was about to close the gap when suddenly a squeal from Olivia intruded on their moment.

"LUCAS!" she screamed, growing louder with her quick approaching steps. He stared at Indie, who crinkled her nose playfully and pushed away from him.

"Hey, bug!" Lucas called back, keeping eye contact with Indie.

"Lucas!" Olivia tackled his leg grabbing on tight. "I wanted to take Indie to see the goats! You took my job," she cried, squeezing his leg and stomping her feet.

"Well, she hasn't met Geraldine," he said, patting her head. Olivia looked up at him, snot dripping down her nose.

"She hasn't?" she asked, wiping her nose.

"I sure haven't," Indie responded, smiling at Olivia.

The three of them returned home covered in dirt from letting Geraldine out of the pen.

Lucas shared the story of Geraldine the 1st and the slap to the face he had experienced and both Olivia and Indie laughed so hard that Indie snorted. Lucas admittedly was worried about his face and had stashed Geraldine in a stall prior to dinner. Unlike the mother and grandmother Geraldine was a perfect lady and nuzzled Indie, until she crouched down to better pet her and then took the opportunity to try and eat her dress. Olivia objected and tried to break the goat and Indie's connection, but only succeeded in knocking both herself and Indie into the dirt. The commotion caught the attention of the other goats, and within seconds, a full stampede was charging their way.

Lucas scooped both girls up and flung them over his shoulder making the way to the exit, everyone laughing.

They walked back into the house to the smell of lemon and lavender. The unmistakable sign that everything had been freshly scrubbed. Charlotte and Daniel were standing outside on the porch watching the setting sun.

"Mom!" Olivia called leaping from Lucas's arms and running up tackling into Charlotte dirt and all. Charlotte laughed, scooping her up and both of them giggled. Lucas glanced over at Daniel leaning in the door frame, rolling his eyes before retreating inside.

"I had such a great time meeting you. I can't wait for you to show me around more next time, Olivia."

Josephine and Hank strolled through the door both smiling as if they had just shared an inside secret.

"So, I see you survived meeting the goats..." Josephine said with a timid tone.

"Yes! They were all so cute and sweet. I can't wait to get to know them more. Maybe I'll pick different clothes next time, though," Indie says with a genuine laugh.

After Indie said her goodbyes, her and Lucas walked awkwardly to her van. Tension and hope in the air.

"I had a great time. Thank you for including me in your family's night," Indie said quickly, feeling a little shy suddenly.

"I'm glad you could make it. I had an amazing time and could tell how much my family adored you," he said, stepping closer to her.

Indie's lips tingled.

Now would be a perfect time to kiss him, she felt her hand reaching up to pull him closer like it was acting on its own. Before she reached for his shirt, Lucas's warm hand embraced hers, breaking the spell. She looked up, meeting his eyes, trying to hold in her laughter as Lucas's ears turned red as he shook her hand. She stepped back, breaking the connection.

"Until next time, farmer boy." Indie gave him a wink before climbing into the van.

So you are on Geraldine the 3rd, but you just call her Geraldine?

That is correct.

She's like the Queen goat you should probably use her full name.

Umm…

Geraldine Moo-donna Carrington the 3rd obviously.

You know goats don't really moo.

I'm no Goat expert.

Don't worry, I'll teach you.

NICOLE LINETTE

Only the Night Owls Know

NICOLE LINETTE

Chapter Twenty-Two

Indie

Indie opened her van door, taking in the crisp night air. It filled her lungs and sent a wave of goosebumps down her arms. Usually, she felt comfort and joy as soon as she set foot into her small home. Tonight was different, though. She felt lonely for the first time in years. Something was missing... she had the startling realization that she wanted to be with Lucas. She wanted family time. This feeling felt foreign to her.

She lets herself imagine what life would be like if she sold her van and settled down here in Deer Isle. Let herself imagine what it would be like to wake up next to Lucas every morning and do farm chores together. To have family meals like tonight every day. The thought brought warmth to her heart. She could definitely imagine this life.

The warm feeling and daydream were soon washed away by a wave of despair. Trusting people enough to stay anywhere long term was not who she was. Time and time again had proven that people would abandon her the moment something or someone else came along.

The thought quickly turned to panic. She had never trusted anyone not to leave her. At least not since her mother died.

She paces around for a while, thinking about what to do. Does she give in to temptation and reach out to Lucas? Her body and heart said yes, but her mind and her defenses screamed no.

Her phone ringing broke her thoughts, causing her to jump in surprise, Eleanor's name showed on the screen. She had forgotten that Eleanor had called her the other day. Eleanor ebbed and flowed just like Indie; she was as close to family as Indie had, and even with Eleanor, she kept herself at arm's length. Joy still washed over her when she thought of Eleanor. Indie felt a sense of comfort knowing that if/when Eleanor disappeared into the wind, they would both be okay; she was prepared and thus not have her heart broken.

Indie: Hi, Eleanor! Sorry, I didn't return your call earlier. Is everything okay?

Eleanor: Oh, honey, don't worry, life escapes us sometimes. I know your last postcard said you were headed to Deer Isle, Maine. I am in Asheville, NC. I know it isn't very close, but I am on the right side of the country for now and would love it if you wanted to visit for a couple of weeks. I can reserve you a spot at the farmers' markets here in town and have a spot for you to hook up your van and trailer.

Indie: You couldn't have called at a better time. I will definitely be there. I'm itching to make a drive. I'll wrap up here and let you know when I'm on the way.

Eleanor: Perfect, see you soon, honey.

Indie hung up the phone. Her phone calls with Eleanor were always brief and to the point, but their in-person conversation ran deep. Indie felt a weight lift from her as she thought of hitting the open road. She grabbed her map and laid it on the picnic table, tracing the route with her finger. This was a newer map, still glossy, the creases crisp. Her older maps with routine outlined and spotted with notes sat in a basket. The maps were pieces of her history, and she protected them as if she were keeping them to be preserved in a museum. A small stab in her heart, forcing her to send a quick message about lunch tomorrow to Sloane. Sloane responded quickly as always, and Indie smiled as peace washed over her.

I have some news… lunch tomorrow?

Definitely. It better be good news.

NICOLE LINETTE

Chapter Twenty-Three

Lucas lay awake in his bed at midnight, and not an ounce of sleep found him. He relived almost brushing his lips against Indie's; he thought of how she would taste. He imagined pulling her into him and grabbing her hair; it would probably feel like silk against his rough hands. He felt himself starting to get worked up thinking about her. With a deep sigh, he climbed from bed, as images of stripping her clothes off started to form. Before he could talk himself out of it, he was grabbing his truck keys and headed to her.

Lucas pulled into Indie's camping spot, and it hit him how startled she might be with him just showing up at 1:00 in the morning. He quickly fired a text to her.

> Are you up?

He heard the soft ping of her phone from the empty hammock and sighed, a disbelieving smile tugging at his lips. Shaking his head, he retrieved it, the screen still glowing from his message, and made his way to the trailer door.

He knocked softly. "Indie? It's Lucas," he called, heart pounding in anticipation.

Before he could even consider stepping back, the door flung open and there she was; even in the dark she radiated, as if she'd been waiting for him. Their eyes met for a heartbeat and then she jumped into his arms wrapping her legs around his waist. He staggered back a half step, catching himself with one hand against the trailer. Her fingers found the back of his head, threading through his hair, pulling him in until their lips collided. Time seemed to stop, the kiss was deep, hungry, and full. Her mouth moved against his like she was memorizing him. She pressed close to his body. He kissed her back fiercely, one hand wrapping around her waist the other getting lost in her hair. Her skin sent waves of warmth through him, her breath was sweet like the season's finest batch of honey.

His instincts drove him to step into her trailer, he stumbled over the entry trying to maintain his grasp while ducking through the door. Indie pulled back looking at him, her lips glistened from their kiss. He felt increased pressure in his pants, and heat crossed his face when her eyes lit up as if she could sense him growing for her. He stood frozen. She unwrapped her legs from him, gently stepping back on the floor. Lucas kept his arms around her waist afraid he'd wake up from this dream if he let go. The sound of blood rushed into his ears as her fingertips ran along the top of his pants. He loosened his grip, giving her room to slide her hands down his torso and over the waistband of his sweatpants, her fingers tracing the edge. She kept her eyes on his face as she moved. He drew in a slow breath, shivering at the feel of her warm, soft hands gliding over his skin. "I couldn't sleep," he whispered.

"Me neither," she responded, running her hand down his pants. He hissed in pleasure, but grabbed her wrist stopping her.

"We don't, you don't, have to." He stumbled, his manhood already kicking him for stopping her.

"I don't mind." The words slapped him in the face. He wanted her to want him, not to tolerate him. Fear washed over him, what if she just wanted to get him out of her system like Lauren said.

"I mind." He pulled her hand up, giving it a kiss before gently picking her up and strolling towards her bed. Her face looked confused, maybe hurt. He fought to keep his resolve.

Lucas cradled her with one arm, her arms holding around his neck. He pulled back the covers and climbed into the bed with her, resting on his chest. She stretched her body out, fitting perfectly against him, even with his pounding erection.

She didn't say anything, but Lucas could sense the questions running through her mind. He brushed her hair back from her face, looking down at her.

"I really like you. We don't need to rush, there's time," he soothed. She smiled shyly and nestled down into him, closing her eyes. Lucas let his eyes fall closed.

Chapter Twenty-Four

She felt her body tense up from the rejection. Her mind kept racing with different thoughts. Past trauma and her abandonment wounds stirred inside her. She started pacing her breath to encourage her pounding heart to slow:

Breathe in for four seconds,

Hold for four seconds,

Release for four seconds,

Hold for four seconds.

She continued her box breathing until the tension started to melt away and her heart started to slow. She focused on the feeling of Lucas's arms around her, warm and comforting. As if he could sense her uneasiness while he slept, she felt him pull her in closer. He was just slowing things down, she thought, not pushing her away. Slow was good, slow was safe, was her final thought as she let her eyes drift close.

The last thing she heard before falling asleep was Lucas's sleepy, soft voice, "I really like you. We don't need to rush; there's time."

Chapter Twenty-Five

Lucas

Lucas gently rolled from Indie's bed; he felt refreshed even with the cramped space. He looked over at Indie. She looked peaceful, her hair spread out over the bed like vines climbing a house. He peeked in on Bambi, who seemed to be staring at him with accusation. "Don't give me that face, nothing happened," he whispered before heading out the door.

Lucas walked into the small coffee shop, the smell of fresh grounds greeting him.

"Lucas, hey man, I feel like I've seen more of you lately, you got a girl now or something?" the barista joked, moving to stand behind the till.

"Or something," he responded, trying to keep his normal expression, but he could feel a smile forming. He hoped that he got the girl, that running to surprise her with coffee and treats would become part of who he was. That one day, he would walk in, and the barista would say: "Picking up something for Indie?"

Lucas made quick work of getting tea and coffee. He picked up some donuts and made his way back to Indie. He was placing the items on the picnic table when Indie emerged from the trailer. He was so caught up in the moment last night, he didn't realize she was in only a long shirt. How easy he could have slid his hands up her, tracing her black underwear that was barely visible. He shoved the thought down.

"Oh, breakfast." She walked over to him, grabbing his shirt and pulling him down for a kiss before sitting at the table. He felt as if he had not stopped smiling. Indie smiled at him, reading the cups and choosing a drink.

"What are your plans today?" she asked while taking a slow sip of tea.

"I planned to do a loop around the farm today, to see if the farm hands need anything. I have a couple of goats I need to assess." He shrugged. "What about you?" He felt like she was growing uneasy.

"Oh, lunch with Sloane, then I need to work on packing up." She spoke so softly he thought he misheard.

"You're leaving? Like leaving Maine or this campsite?" He felt his heart drop.

"Just for a bit, a friend of mine is in Asheville, North Carolina. It's about a 19-hour drive, so I figured I got to see her for a bit, there's a market down there." She seemed to be rambling.

"Do you plan to..." he paused, rotating the cup in his hand, "do you plan to come back after?"

"Yeah, I don't think I'm done here. I still have places I'm hoping to explore." He let out a sigh of relief.

"Okay, well, I'll be here when you get back, but maybe you can keep me updated while you're gone. I would be interested in learning more about your travels." She smiled at his words.

"I would be delighted to share photos with you. Oh, you could follow my Instagram and see my past adventures too." She patted the spot next to her. Lucas sat down, and over the next hour, he watched as Indie's eyes danced with joy, reliving some of her favorite experiences while showing him photos.

As if she could sense that he had to start his day, Indie set her phone down. "Sorry, I sort of got derailed. It's nice to share these memories with someone." Lucas studied her blushing face.

"I love hearing your stories." He paused. "Your memories are worth sharing. I should probably make my way to work, though." Even though he didn't want to go, he held out his arms embracing her as she stepped in. He kissed the top of her head. "Text me," he whispered, letting the hug linger a little longer before stepping back.

On the drive home he wondered if he made a mistake stopping Indie last night. What if she left and never came back? He just had to trust that she wasn't done here, and she would return to him.

He pulled up next to the barn, pulling his phone out and he dialed Lauren. Lauren answered on the first ring.

"Hey man, what's up?" His voice sounded concerned, how often had Lucas called him lately, obviously not enough, if Lauren thought this could be an emergency.

"Hey, I need some advice..." Lucas tried to keep his voice neutral.

"Oh, okay, yeah, let's hear it, I am a great advice giver." Lauren laughed through the phone.

"Indie is leaving to visit someone in Asheville and I'm wanting to give her a reason to come back as soon as possible. I've been enjoying getting to know her and feel like there's more..." He trailed off.

"You're worried she's going to leave and not come back? Did she say she'd come back?"

"She said she wasn't done here, but I feel like, I don't know, like if she decided in the spur of the moment she would not come back." Lucas could hear Lauren humming.

"Tell her you won't fuck her until she gets back." Lucas grunted in response. Lauren let out a laugh. "I'm just fucking with you, I know that's not how you roll." There was a pause that seemed to drag on forever. "Maybe plan a trip for the two of you since she loves traveling?" Lucas thought about it for a minute.

"Okay yeah I could do that, thanks." He quickly hung up the phone, not waiting for Lauren's reply.

Dang, not even a goodbye.

You're welcome.

Lucas didn't respond to Lauren; his brain was already making a plan.

Let me take you to Portland, Maine, when you get back.

I haven't been there in years, and I have never really explored outside work so maybe you can show me how truly visiting a place is done.

Indie responded quickly:

I would like that, it's a date.

Lucas smiled; it felt like he grasped a small tangible piece of Indie and he was determined to keep a hold.

Chapter Twenty-Six

Indie smiled. How long has it been since she made plans for the future that she was excited about? She tucked her phone away, pulling into Sloane's driveway. The house shone with even more grace in the sunlight than it did in the moonlight.

Music flowed from the house, and Indie could hear Sloane singing along to Gorgeous by Taylor Swift. Indie walked through the screen door, spotting Sloane in the kitchen, twirling around. Butterscotch was sleeping in the window above the sink, unbothered by the noise.

Indie leaned agains the doorway watching her for a moment.

Sloane twirled by Butterscotch, giving his butt a scratch. Indie joined in singing and twirling into the kitchen. Sloane jumped in surprise but fell right back into her dance. They were both laughing by the time the song finished.

"Let's take lunch on the back porch." Sloane grabbed the charcuterie board, and Indie grabbed the pitcher of drinks.

"WOW, you outdid yourself," Indie responded, looking at the platter in Sloane's hands.

"Girl, I don't cook. I ordered this, all I did was organize it on the tray." She laughed, pushing open the back door. The backyard was amazing, a long green yard with a single tree towards the back. Flowerpots lined the covered deck. Garden beds followed the fences. String lights hanging, emanating a warm glow.

"Sloane, your backyard is amazing," Indie breathed, taking in the scent of the flowers.

"Oh yeah, it has taken some time, but I've really learned to embrace flower growing. Funny, right cause I grow them and you dry them." She laughed, sitting down at the small table. "You know if you're ever short on flowers, I have plenty." Indie sat down, pouring the drinks.

"That's awesome, thank you. You know I was at Lucas's last night for dinner."

"Yes, girl, tell me everything," Sloane squealed. Indie playfully rolled her eyes.

"His family was funny, it was a great time, but what I was getting at is that they have the cutest goats and even have some young ones." Sloane waved her hand like she was boring her.

"Yes, yes, we all know about his vicious goats." Sloane chuckled.

"They are sweet goats," Indie corrected before moving on. "Anyways, they also have a grass field by the goats that you could totally do goat yoga in."

Sloane paused, holding a cracker with cheese close to her mouth. She sat it down, drumming her fingers on the table.

"You know that could be fun. I was trying to find a way to branch out. Let's do it! Maybe you can embroider some sweat towels for me like Pose and Petals: Goat Yoga, with a cute little goat. Can you do that?" Sloane spoke quickly, the idea exciting her.

"I can, in about two to four weeks," Indie said softly, smiling at Sloane. Sloane stopped her smile, fading into a frown.

"Why four months? Why so long? I can't believe you're leaving me." She stood up and started to pace around the deck.

"Sloane, it's only four weeks max, I promise. I can totally work on some merch while I'm gone."

Sloane stopped moving and put her hands on her hips. "Well, four weeks is a lot less time, but I'm still not happy about it."

She sat back down, taking Indie's hand. "You have to promise to text me so I will know you're okay." Indie nodded, the words caught in her throat. She wanted to tell Sloane this wasn't her permanent home and that someday, probably soon, she would move on. "Indie, you have to promise."

Indie cleared her throat. "Yes, I promise I will keep you updated. Then, when I get back, we will have the best goat yoga day." Indie returned Sloane's slowly growing smile.

"Okay, then we don't have a problem. I thought I was going to have to kidnap you. I just figured out how to take care of a cat, I don't think I'm ready for a prisoner, yet." She laughed.

Giddy like a Gilmore

NICOLE LINETTE

Chapter Twenty-Seven

Indie

After a few days of being on the road, driving through countless states, Indie finally slowed her pace. She stopped in Salem, Massachusetts, just long enough to soak in the witchy vibes, wandering cobblestone streets lined with crooked shop signs and the faint smell of cinnamon from a bakery. She let the aura fuel her creativity, and she drew out plans for harvest-themed soaps and wreaths.

In Connecticut, she couldn't resist pulling into the quaint town that had inspired her comfort fall show Gilmore Girls. Standing in the middle of the town square, she smiled to herself. Maybe Lucas could be her Luke. The thought caused a pull at her heartstrings for not just Lucas, but for Sloane as well.

She pulled into Asheville, rolling down the windows and taking in the fresh mountain air. She pulled out her phone and sent Sloane a text letting her know she made it. Like she promised, attaching a photo of the "Welcome to North Carolina" sign.

Next she fired off a text to Lucas.

She had sent them pictures from every state she'd passed through, each one with its own quirky caption. She felt a surprising warmth in her chest; she'd never had anyone to share moments like this with before. Usually, her pictures stayed in her camera roll or were seen only by the few people who watched her Instagram stories.

She knocked on Eleanor's door and as if Eleanor sensed her pulling up the door flung open and she was swept into a bear hug.

Eleanor looked older, and more fragile than Indie remembered, a sight that sent a sharp wave of guilt through her. It had been too long.

After her mother passed, Eleanor was one of the few adults who offered her steady love and support. She came to see her as the grandmother she had never had.

Indie's mind drifted to the first time they'd met.

She had been sitting on the front porch of her foster home, admiring the neighbor's flower garden. Flowers and bursts of color had always brought her joy. Eleanor had stepped outside to tend to her blooms, noticed the young girl watching, and called out a gentle "Hello." She'd asked if Indie wanted to help water and trim the flowers. Eleanor had a big straw hat on and bright pink gardening gloves, and was in a pair of old overalls. Maybe it was the outfit or maybe the tone, but Indie's alarm bells didn't sound, and back then they rang non-stop.

From that day on, it became a daily ritual, the highlight of Indie's afternoons. It was safety and peace in her chaotic uncertain life. Even now, she could close her eyes and smell the soft sweetness of peonies drifting on the summer air.

"Indie?" Eleanor's voice pulled her back.

"Oh sorry. I was lost in thoughts," Indie said with a small smile. "I remember the outfit you wore when I met you." Indie glanced Eleanor over. "It pretty much looked just like this." She laughed.

Eleanor's eyes crinkled warmly, and she made a tsk sound before lightly thumping Indie with her pink gardening glove.

"Come on, I just put the tea in the garden. I want to know all about Maine. How has it been? Have you met anyone yet? A friend...? Maybe someone that's more than a friend?" Eleanor gave her a wink, like she could sense some sort of change in Indie since arriving in Maine. Indie followed her through the house.

"I have made a great friend named Sloane. I've also maybe met someone... but I'm not sure where to go with that yet." Indie found herself excited to share, not about her markets but about the people.

Eleanor's knowing look softened. "I know in the past you've been let down, and it's scary to let somebody in. Don't push away love and friendship because of the past." She patted Indie's shoulder and took a seat at the table.

The evening was filled with reconnection. Eleanor shared stories of her youth, love and loss, as if she was trying to push Indie out of her comfort zone. Indie went to bed feeling at ease and looking forward to her time with Eleanor, she didn't realize how much she missed her.

The next morning, Eleanor suggested they spend the day at Biltmore Estate, and Indie instantly agreed. The drive through the winding mountain roads was peaceful, the kind of ride where conversation came easily, and the scenery felt like it could heal something inside you.

When they arrived, the grand estate rose before them like something out of a fairytale, its stone facade glowing gold in the morning light. Indie paused on the gravel path, taking it all in: the turrets, the sprawling lawns, the scent of freshly cut grass mingling with faint sweetness from the nearby gardens. She wondered how to capture this moment in a creation.

They wandered slowly through the house, Indie listening with fascination as Eleanor pointed out her favorite rooms, the library with its rolling ladders, the sun-dappled solarium, the dining hall that seemed too grand for any real family meal. Indie found herself imagining Lucas here, leaning against the banister of the grand staircase, looking at her like he was taking her all in and trying to absorb her.

Her phone buzzed in her pocket.

Did you make it to the giant castle yet?

It's a mansion. But yes. Feels like I should've worn a ball gown.

You'd look good in one.

And what would you wear?

Flannel. Obviously.

Ran into Sloane. She mentioned Goat Yoga?

She bit her lip to hide a smile, tucking the phone away before Eleanor could notice her cheeks warming.

After touring the house, they stepped into the gardens. The air was warmer now, filled with the hum of bees and the rustle of leaves. Rows of roses in shades of blush and cream swayed gently in the breeze. Eleanor walked a few steps ahead, her fingers grazing petals as if greeting old friends. Indie followed, letting the moment wash over her, the peace of the mountains, the comfort of being with someone who felt like home.

The roses stirred another memory. She was fourteen, living in her fourth house with a foster family who preferred she stay invisible. The house was cold, the air thick with rules she couldn't seem to follow. One evening, after another silent dinner, she'd walked the hour walk to Eleanor's and found her kneeling in the dirt, pulling weeds. Without a word, Eleanor had patted the ground beside her. They worked in quiet harmony until Eleanor poured them each a glass of lemonade, the kind with pulp, and told her, "Sometimes, flowers grow best after they've been cut back." Indie didn't know if she was talking about roses or about her. She still didn't.

They found a shaded bench overlooking a fountain, where they shared a small picnic. Eleanor had packed fresh bread, cheese, grapes, and a thermos of homemade sweet tea. They talked about nothing and everything: old memories, silly stories from the road, even a few half-joking questions about this mysterious man in Maine. Every time Lucas's name came up, Eleanor's lips twitched knowingly, and Indie pretended not to notice.

As they walked back toward the car, Indie glanced once more at the roses swaying in the breeze. Maybe Eleanor had been right all those years ago; maybe she was just another flower learning how to grow after being cut back. And maybe, this time, she was ready to bloom.

Chapter Twenty-Eight

Lucas

Lucas drummed his fingers on the steering wheel. He watched out the window as his mother examined a dresser she was hoping to buy. The house he was parked outside was painted a light yellow and seemed to blend into the hay field behind it. The house was a stark contrast to the dark barn next to it, the roof slightly sunken, paint peeling, but the wall looked sturdy, even with the vines taking it over. It was as if the world moved around the barn, leaving it to fend on its own. He wondered if, as a foster child, that was Indie's experience. The world was shifting around her as she struggled to find her place.

The tap on the driver's window startled Lucas out of his thoughts. He smiled at his mother as he rolled down the window.

"I think this is the dresser. Can you help me load it up?" Josephine seemed to give him a knowing smile. As if she could sense that his thoughts were on Indie.

"Yeah, sounds good. Glad you like this is the dresser." He climbed from the truck, walking towards the man.

"Oh, you are just tired of driving me around to find a dresser," she responded, following him.

"Never," Lucas called over his shoulder, reaching out his hand to the man, "Greg." Greg reached for his hand.

"Lucas, good to see you again. Hope everything is going well." Greg was a short, stocky man with stark black hair despite his older age.

"I can't complain." Lucas gave him a smile before grabbing one side of the dresser. His phone sounded, the alert signaling a text from Indie. He fought the urge to check his phone.

"Come on, boys, let's load the dresser up so I can get home and start my project." Josephine clapped her hands with joy.

"You, Josephine, always have some project up your sleeve. I'm excited to see what you do to this old dresser."

As Lucas pulled the truck off the gravel road, Josephine cleared her throat. "You know I went on a couple of dates with Greg once," she said, glancing at him.

"Oh?" Lucas didn't remember his mother ever speaking of Greg.

"Yeah, only a couple of dates. You know Greg was a foster kid. I mean, he had aged out of the system before we went out." She let the word hang between them.

"Okay..." Lucas wasn't sure where she was going with this conversation.

"I'm not saying this to deter you, or to discredit anyone's experiences, but I just want you to be sensitive to what Indie might have experienced."

"I don't think I understand what you mean? What happened between you and Greg?" Lucas pulled over on a gravel pull-off so he could focus on his mom.

"Well, believe it or not, I was sort of flaky." She gave a small chuckle. "When I was nineteen, I was, let's say, a little wild. I was figuring myself out and was definitely not in a place to be predictable. I think it was hard for Greg not to know when or if I was coming and going, and I think it caused some trauma response. We... well, we had a few tense moments." Josephine's smile fell into something more reflective. "Nothing dramatic. But if I ran late or didn't answer right away, he'd shut down. Or he'd get prickly, like he was bracing for something bad. At the time. I thought it meant we weren't a good match. Two people at totally different points in life. I didn't understand what he was actually reacting to."

Lucas watched her twist her wedding band, the gold warm and familiar on her finger.

"I didn't realize until years later that my flakiness wasn't just inconvenient for him," she continued softly. "It fed some old wounds. Ones I didn't cause, but one's I accidentally poked at anyway."

Lucas's grip on the steering wheel tightened. "You think Indie...?"

"I think," Josephine said gently, "that people who grew up without stability often feel things a little sharper. Even if they're strong. Even if they're the sunniest person you've ever met."

Indie's laugh flickered in his mind. Bright and wild. But he also pictured the way she'd gone quiet that day in the field, the tiny flicker of uncertainty she tried to hide when plans shifted.

"I'm not warning you off," Josephine added quickly. "I adore that girl. I'm just saying... be steady with her. Be clear. Show up when you say you will. It matters more than you might realize."

Lucas swallowed, a knot forming in his chest. "I do show up."

"I know you do." She reached over and squeezed his wrist. "Just... remember she may read between the lines more than most. If she ever seems scared or pulls back, it might not be about you. It might be echoes of old things."

He nodded slowly. The truck hummed around them, the only sound for a moment.

"Don't get me wrong," Josephine said, brightening, "your father is my soulmate, and I don't think I could ever be as truly happy with someone else. Greg and I weren't meant to be. But that little time taught me something important. Sometimes the kindest thing we can do for someone is give them the stability we've always taken for granted."

Lucas took a breath, starting to drive again. "Yeah," he murmured, Indie's unread text burning a quiet hole in his pocket. "I hear you."

NICOLE LINETTE

Boom Went the Flower Bud

NICOLE LINETTE

Chapter Twenty-Nine

Indie

The rain tapped against the roof of the trailer like a quiet metronome, steady and soft. Indie sat cross-legged on her bed, a mug of chamomile cooling beside her, the familiar little leather journal Eleanor had given her balanced in her lap.

Her mother had gotten her into writing, and she had loved sharing key memories in the journal to read back to her mother in the evenings. They would curl together under the blankets with their books, and the rest of the world would melt away.

The sweet thought faded from her as she remembered coming home to her last placement to see one of the other kids digging through her things.

The anger that filled her when they tossed the journal, dried flowers, and pictures falling from the pages, petals crumbling on the floor. She had quickly snatched it up and run to Eleanor's. She could feel the ache in her throat. She had left the journal with her for safekeeping, and even with prompting, Indie had never been able to touch it again. It was like the sweet memories of her youth were wrapped in thorns, and any time she thought of touching it, her skin burned. Today was different, though the thought of holding it sent waves of warmth and good memories.

"Okay, Bambi, let me read you a story," she whispered, staring at her little friend before opening the book.

The pages smelled faintly of lavender and dust, and the delicate, looping handwriting inside was hers but not quite hers. This was the voice of a girl who hadn't yet been broken.

She ran her fingers over the faded purple ink: one of the last entries from a lifetime ago.

March 12th,

"Today, Mom said we could go to the spring fair after school. She promised we could ride the Ferris wheel twice, once for the view and once to make silly faces at the people on the ground. I told her I'd win her a stuffed animal from the ring toss, even though I've never won anything. She laughed and said she didn't care if I won or not, because she already had me. I tried to roll my eyes, but my cheeks hurt from smiling. Her perfume smelled like vanilla and something flowery like the little garden she always watered by the window."

Indie blinked, the words blurring. She could almost hear her mom's voice, warm, teasing, just a little raspy from too much coffee and late-night talking. She could picture the loose curl falling into her mom's eyes, the soft scrape of her sneakers on the kitchen tiles, the faint hum of the old radio playing a song they both loved.

Her thumb brushed over the next few lines.

"She braided my hair this morning. Said I should look like a princess for the fair, even if my crown is a little crooked. She said I'll always be her best girl. I told her she was my best girl, too. She laughed so hard she dropped her hairbrush. I could still smell the warmth of her shampoo as she leaned over me, the cinnamon scent from breakfast lingering in the air. Everything felt golden this morning, like magic in the sunlight through the window."

A laugh slipped from Indie now, but it caught in her throat halfway out. She could see the small kitchen, the chipped blue mug in her mom's hand, the faint sticky sweetness of strawberry jam on the counter. The memory was so vivid it was almost cruel.

She turned the page.

The handwriting changed, shaky, hurried, jagged where the pen had pressed too hard.

"The sirens were loud today. A lady I didn't know came to my classroom and told me I had to come with her. She wouldn't tell me why. I thought maybe I was in trouble. She walked me to the nurse's office, but Mom wasn't there. Just another lady with sad eyes. She said 'honey' too many times, like she was trying to make it soft. She said my mom had an accident. She said she was gone. I said no. I said she couldn't be gone because she was waiting for me at the fair. She had to be. She promised. I can still smell the vanilla of her perfume from yesterday and the cinnamon from breakfast. How can all that sweetness be gone already?"

Indie's breath hitched. She clutched the journal like it might keep her from falling apart.

"I kept asking if she was sure. She didn't answer. She just put her hand on my shoulder and started crying too. I wanted to run to the fair. I thought maybe if I got there first, she'd still be there, holding two tickets for the Ferris wheel and smiling like she always did when she saw me. But they wouldn't let me go. They kept saying, 'We'll take care of you now.' I don't want them to take care of me. I just want my mom."

The next several pages were shaky words scratched out; she couldn't make out the words or remember what she wrote, but she could remember the feeling of panic and fear, followed by numbness and disbelief. The camper felt too small, too still. The sound of the wind outside seemed far away, muffled by the weight in her chest. She could almost hear the faint creak of the Ferris wheel in her memory, the soft clinking of the fair's tin cups, the distant murmur of laughter that had been hers and her mom's only.

Indie closed the journal slowly, but the ache stayed—like an echo from twelve years old that had never really faded. She pressed the leather to her face, inhaling its faint lavender scent as if it could somehow reach the memory of her mom.

She wiped at her cheeks with the heel of her hand, but more tears kept coming. The past and present swirled together, and for a moment, she let herself sink fully into the grief, the love, and the sweetness that had been stolen too soon. The energy drained from her; she felt like she should have read more, but couldn't bring herself to. She set the journal on the table and grabbed her phone.

So goat yoga…

NICOLE LINETTE

Chapter Thirty

Lucas

Lucas stacked the last crate of honey on the shelf, the sharp scent of them lingering in the air. The market had been open for hours, but the post-day cleanup always felt longer than the selling itself. Charlotte was wiping down the counter, humming something upbeat under her breath.

"What's got you smiling like that?" she asked without looking up.

"I'm not smiling."

"You're grinning like Otis when he got into the strawberry bush," she said, tossing the rag on the counter. "Let me guess...it has something to do with a certain redhead?"

Lucas's hands stilled on the crate. "Maybe." He was thankful Charlotte was able to attend the market at the last minute with him. It distracted him from constantly checking for a message from Indie.

Charlotte leaned against the counter, eyes dancing. "Spill it. What's going on?"

Lucas tried to keep it casual. "Indie, she just..." He hesitated, running a hand over the back of his neck. "She... she makes things feel easy. Free."

Charlotte's smile widened. "Free. I like that word for you. Do you remember how free the farmers' market used to feel when we were kids?"

Lucas gave her a look. "Define 'free.'"

"You know, running wild between stalls, swiping free samples like little bandits, chasing each other until Mom yelled. Dancing barefoot to whatever band was playing by the fountain." She laughed softly, the sound tinged with nostalgia. "Those Saturdays were magic."

He shook his head. "That's not what I remember."

Charlotte frowned. "Really?"

"Really. I remember waking up before dawn to load the truck. Counting cash at the register while you were off getting sticky from the kettle corn. Making sure Dad's signs didn't blow away in the wind. I wasn't running around. I was keeping the market running."

Charlotte tilted her head. "You were eight, Lucas."

"And you were eleven," he laughed and then paused, "somebody had to make sure it didn't fall apart."

For a moment, the only sound was the hum of the cooler.

"You know," Lucas said slowly, "with Indie... it felt like I finally got to be the kid you were back then. Not the one holding everything together. Just... someone having fun."

Charlotte's expression softened. "All that joy from taking her around the farm. The place you grew up in."

Charlotte studied him for a long moment. "You know you don't have to wait for someone else to give you permission to have fun, to be free?"

"Maybe," he said. "But it's easier when someone's standing there, daring you to try."

His smile turned knowing. "Sounds like she's good for you. I'm glad you are finally seeing the fun the farm can be."

Lucas busied himself with stacking the last of the produce, but he didn't argue.

That night, Lucas lay in bed trying to figure out how Charlotte could remember the fun, but he only remembered the work. One of his earliest memories that was clouded by time came back to him. He was maybe six and trying to sneak down to the kitchen for some fresh strawberries after bed. He was right outside the kitchen when he heard his parents enter from the porch. They spoke quietly but in an angry tone.

"I just think we need more help," Josephine whispered.

"I already told you, Jo, we can't afford it. Not with... you know," Hank responded. Lucas wanted to go back upstairs, but he kept listening.

"He is the reason we need more help. I won't be able to do everything I'm doing and care for him."

"You did in the past."

"Hank, I was younger." His mother's voice rose, then lowered to a more comforting tone. "Your parents could do more back then."

Lucas retreated, not wanting to hear more. Were they talking about him? He didn't mean to spill the jug of goat milk that morning; he just wanted to play and not wait for his mom to help him. Tears welled in his eyes. He didn't want his mom and dad to fight. He was going to be the best worker, then his mom wouldn't have to care for him, and they wouldn't have to hire anyone.

He remembered making sure his chores were done without being asked, and helping Charlotte do hers. He helped wherever he could, and he made sure not to make a mistake; they couldn't afford him to make a mistake. He vaguely had an image of Charlotte dancing around the yard with flowers in her hair, almost identical to Olivia. She waved to him from the window, trying to get him to come outside. He had waved back, but didn't leave the barn. His mother told him to play, but he didn't have time for that anymore.

Lucas turned over in bed, the old ache curling back into his chest. That may be the difference. Charlotte remembered the sunshine, the laughter, the scent of warm bread, and chasing chickens around the coop. He remembered the heavy pail in his arms and the daunting pressure to work harder.

He wasn't angry at the memories Charlotte had, but he did wish she had noticed how hard he had to work to be what his family needed. He carried this guilt that if he couldn't keep up, the farm would fail. Maybe that is why he felt so uneasy with the fact that there were new farmhands and equipment running the farm.

His phone pinged, breaking his thoughts. He smiled at Indie's name.

So goat yoga…

Yes, goat yoga.

It would be best if I call you.

You can always call me.

His phone started to ring, and relief washed over him.

City Lights & Open Hearts

NICOLE LINETTE

Chapter Thirty-One

Lucas

The bed of Lucas's truck was stacked neatly, a small cooler wedged into the corner, and a folded blanket tossed on top for good measure. He ran through his mental checklist, finding it hard to concentrate; his mind wasn't on the sunscreen or rain jackets. It was on her. She had been gone for what felt like years, and he couldn't wait to see her face again. They had talked every night on the phone since that first call, and the memory of her voice now lulled him to sleep every night. While excitement burst from him, he also felt a small tremor of anxiety.

He'd booked the hotel room as soon as she said yes to joining. A little impulsively for him, knowing Indie was more of a pull-over-when-the-mood-strikes kind of girl. He'd even hovered over the "confirm" button longer than he cared to admit, feeling like once he clicked it, there was no turning back. The reservation felt... concrete. Unmovable. Which was exactly the opposite of her style.

Still, he wanted to show her off, watch her face as she saw the sidewalks lit up at night, enjoy dinners that stretched for hours, and mornings spent in coffee shops where the smell of fresh espresso hung in the air. All the things his sister boasted about when he had told her of his plan to take Indie to Portland.

Her laugh had started to live in his head rent-free. That loose, unfiltered sound. And her smile, bright in a way that seemed to soften every rigid edge he'd built into his life. For the first time in years, he let his mind wander from the farm and work. He imagined them moving from one place to another, maybe her camper parked next to his truck, sunsets blurring into new mornings. The thought didn't scare him.

It made him excited. He looked up the road, spotting a small cloud of dust with purple peeking through. Indie was almost to him, his pulse quickened, and his pants tightened.

Chapter Thirty-Two

When Lucas told her to pack for a few days, she'd pictured some cozy coastal town, not this. Portland sprawled out in a patchwork of brick buildings, cobblestone streets, and the tang of saltwater in the air. She leaned forward in her seat, eyes darting from one colorful storefront to the next.

"You've been holding out on me," she teased, pressing her palm to the glass like she might leave a print behind. "I thought we were going fishing or something, but this... this is fancy."

"Fishing is fancy," he deadpanned, glancing at her with that crooked smirk that always made her stomach flip. "You just have questionable taste."

"Oh, please," she shot back. "If you think worms and bait count as fancy, I'm a five-star chef."

She was full of anticipation and had been from the moment she pulled back into Deer Isle. She had found herself searching the sidewalks, trying to spot Lucas, knowing he was probably on the farm. Indie almost forgot to stop by Sloane's; that's how clouded her mind was of him. She made no unnecessary stops on the drive back; she let the memories of his laugh and the feel of her hands on him to keep her momentum and banish distractions. Sloane, of course, was ecstatic to see her, but could sense her unrest. She had reluctantly shooed Indie away with the reminder to text her everything.

The Hotel lobby was sleek but warm, with big leather chairs and a wall of windows framing the skyline. "So... we're staying here?" she asked, turning toward him with wide eyes. She rarely did hotels, and when she did, they were not nearly this fancy.

"Yeah," he said, and there was a flicker of uncertainty in his grin like he wasn't sure she'd like it. She realized this trip was a little outside his norm, too, and that he'd thought about it, planned it, for her. That mattered more than the skyline.

"Maybe fishing is fancy." She winked at him as she watched the receptionist hand him two keys, which he fumbled. "Easy, big fella." She laughed, picking up her bag and leaving a hand free for him.

"I figured we could walk to dinner, maybe hit a few spots, see the city at night," he said, grasping her hand and stepping into the elevator. She leaned back against the mirrored wall, her reflection grinning at him. Her stomach did a little flip thinking of sharing the hotel room with him.

"This is a different side of you. So unstructured."

He shrugged. "Well, sometimes you have to go where the wind takes you."

Her eyebrow arched, and she blushed as they made eye contact in the mirror. Indie wondered if he was implying he would travel with her. She let herself reflect briefly on that thought. She could imagine him driving her van for long stretches of time, his hand resting on her leg and her hand on top of his. The music will fill the comfortable silence, and the wind from the open window will make every moment feel magical. The sound of the elevator brought her back to the moment.

They set their bags down and were immediately drawn to the harbor view outside the window. Indie felt her pulse quicken as she looked at the bed. Part of her wanted to throw him on the bed and strip him right now. She let a shiver pass through her.

"Cold?" Lucas responded by setting his suitcase on the holder. "I brought extra jackets."

"Nope, just excited to see what's in store for the night," she chirped, leaving her bag on the floor and leaving the statement open to interpretation.

The Portland Museum of Art came first, and she drifted from painting to painting, letting the brushstrokes fill her creative mind. Lucas kept up with her, not rushing her or complaining. Occasionally, he would mention something he liked, which she found hilarious because she could feel him staring at her.

Afterward, they wandered toward the water, where fishing boats swayed gently against the docks, their ropes creaking. Occasionally, his hand would brush hers, and she could feel his finger twitch with the anticipation of grabbing hers.

When he suggested a whale-watching tour, she gave a wide, nervous smile, which he seemed to catch. "I've never been on a boat in the ocean before," she confessed, and he looked almost proud to be the one to change that.

On the dock, she tugged the zipper of her jacket up to her chin and tilted her head toward him. "If I get seasick, you have to hold my hair."

"Fair," he said, adjusting the strap of the camera around his neck. "If I get seasick, you have to drive my truck home."

"Oh, absolutely, I might even do it just because." She laughed. Indie looked out over the water. A nervous feeling began to grow in her stomach. Instinctively, her hand reached out and grasped Lucas's. She's been on small bodies of water and on small boats, like kayaks and paddle boards, if those counted, but never on the ocean. It wasn't like she didn't have the opportunity; she just never had the drive. The ocean was like another world, one she could not easily access and grasp. Every time she had almost gone into the ocean, she retreated at the last moment, but maybe this time with Lucas, she could do it.

NICOLE LINETTE

Chapter Thirty-Three

Lucas

On deck, the sea air wrapped around them, briny and cold, and he caught the way she gripped the railing like it might fly away without her. He watched in awe as Indie was able to contain her hair in a bun as the wind whipped it around, and noticed the small tremor in her hands. He was about to reach out to comfort her when a whale surfaced; her gasp cut through the chatter of the other passengers. Her eyes were wide, her knuckles turned white from grasping the rail, and for a second, he forgot to look at the ocean at all.

"I will never understand the ocean," she murmured in awe. Lucas stepped closer, taking the risk of wrapping his arms around her and placing his hands over hers. She seemed to ease at his touch.

"You aren't going to believe me when I say this, but you don't have to understand everything."

Indie laughed, keeping her gaze locked on the ocean.

"That sounds like something Charlotte would have told you."

It filled Lucas with pride that his sister made an impression on Indie.

They ended the evening at Fort Sumner Park, a blanket between them and the grass, their picnic from The Bite Into Maine food truck spread out between them. The Lighthouse's beam swept the water as the sun melted into the horizon.

Lucas reached into his bag and pulled out the small box, handing it to her without a word. His hands itched with anticipation. He wasn't sure if it was too soon for present giving, but it felt right. Indie tilted her head with a questionable look, then gently started to unwrap the brown paper, exposing the small wooden box. He watched her open it slowly; he could swear sweat was building on his back. Indie pulled out the small dark leather notebook with flowers imprinted on the cover. He cleared his throat.

"I saw this, and it reminded me of you."

The way she looked at him was mesmerizing, like he wasn't just a stop along her travels but maybe, just maybe, a place she could stay, which hit him harder than the ocean wind.

He was falling. No, he'd already fallen in love with her, and he knew he couldn't escape it nor would he want to.

Chapter Thirty-Four

Indie held the journal in her palm the whole drive to the hotel. They sat in comfortable silence, as if the day had created a calm peace in them. Indie hooked her arm around his free arm and leaned on his shoulder as he drove them.

"I used to journal all the time," Indie broke the silence. "Like almost daily, my mom said it was one of the easier ways to share and process our experiences. I loved it, I loved how the pen felt on the paper, how she and I could just sit together, both quietly reflecting on the day." She felt Lucas shift in his seat.

"That sounds like a wonderful memory to have with your mom," he responded softly.

"It was, sometimes we would add in pressed flowers, or ticket stubs. It was a running record of our lives."

"Do you still journal?"

"No, not really. I mean, I use journals for concepts of my artwork, but not as like a diary."

"Why did you stop?" She thought about it, really, why had she stopped? Because her mother died and her world shrank so much that there was nothing worth writing? Because every word that spilled from her could be used as a weapon? Silence settled in the truck again, but this time, heavier.

She cleared her throat. "When I was in foster care, it wasn't safe to be connected to something like a journal. The more something meant to you, the more it would hurt having it taken away." She could hear her own voice crack. "But recently…" She paused, glancing up at Lucas, who had pulled the truck over and was watching her. "Recently, I thought that maybe it was something I wanted to start again." She looked down at the journal. Letting her free hand trace the flowers.

"Your words, your stories, your experiences are safe with me," Lucas whispered, shifting in his seat, causing her to shift back to sitting. His hand grazed her cheek before sliding to her chin and lifting her face towards him. Slowly, he kissed her lips, then her forehead. He put the truck in drive before wrapping his arm over her shoulder and pulling her close. Indie let her body relax under his arm, her head leaning on his shoulder as he started back towards the hotel.

By the time they made it back to the hotel, the city's glow had deepened into that quiet, steady hum that only came late at night. Lucas slid the keycard into the door, holding it open so she could step inside first. The room was softly lit, the view of the harbor twinkling beyond the glass.

"Today was one of the best days," she said, walking in and stretching her arms out before setting the journal gently on top of her bag. She turned towards Lucas, who was leaning against the wall, watching her.

"I am glad you enjoyed today," he said, smiling softly. She felt a blush creeping up.

She kicked off her shoes and curled into one of the big armchairs.

"So... do we order dessert?"

"Obviously, we need dessert," he said, their eyes catching. She felt her body tingle in anticipation. She reached for the phone.

"Cheesecake?" She almost choked on her words, keeping his gaze. He nodded quietly. She broke eye contact, looking down at her phone.

"I'm going to take a quick rinse and get into something more comfortable," he said, turning towards the bathroom.

Before she could stop herself, she responded, "I think that's supposed to be my line." He chuckled in response and closed the bathroom door, and she let out a long exhale.

Moving quickly, she ordered the cheesecake and gave her armpits a sniff, making a face. She grabbed her deodorant. Brushed out her hair and changed into a pair of small pajama shorts and an oversized T-shirt. She had just sat down on the bed when Lucas stepped out of the bathroom wearing just shorts.

"Ahh, you got into something comfortable too," he commented, looking her over.

"You too," she replied as he stepped closer to her. Her fingers reached up to feel his abs, and he glanced at her hands, then at her eyes. "You, you didn't put a shirt on," she said, lifting her hands up. "I could tickle you so easily." She danced her fingers towards his abs.

"You wouldn't," he joked. Her legs moved on their own, widening so he could step closer.

"Oh, I would." She stopped her hands with the fingertips brushing his abs. She heard his exhale and looked up at him. He grabbed her wrists, now standing between her legs. She took deep breaths, her body coming alive and her center heating. She could feel moisture gathering in her underwear. She had never been so turned on by a man's chest before.

"I want to scoop you up," he whispered, and she nodded in response. He lifted her, pulling her towards him. She wrapped her legs around his waist and her arms around his neck. He pulled her tight and moved them both onto the bed, laying her head on the pillow. She let her grasp loosen as he hovered over her, creating more space so she could look at him. She licked her lips as an invitation. He entwined his finger in her hair, and she gasped as he let his weight settle on her as he started to kiss her neck. Her hunger for him grew when she felt his erection against her. His other hand slid up her shirt, and she let out a moan in pleasure.

"Your boobs are perfect," he whispered into her neck before kissing her earlobe and then tracing his lips over hers, all while kneading her breasts. "I want to see them." He gasped as her hand trailed up his sides, then down his stomach, starting to trace along his shorts.

"I'm getting so hot," she whispered, "I think I need to lose a layer," she tried to joke. He sat up, straddling her. He watched as she lifted her shirt slowly, exposing her shorts, then her stomach, and finally removed the entire shirt, exposing her chest. Her nipples hummed from the attention as he stared at her.

"I just want to be clear," he said breathlessly, "clear on how far you want to go." He let out a moan as she grasped his erection through his shorts.

"I want to feel this inside me," she said, giving his penis a squeeze. He groaned, pressing his hips forward and leaning down to trace her nipples with his tongue.

Indie hummed with pleasure as his mouth and hands explored her body, slowly taking off her shorts and sliding his tongue down her clit. She gasped, grabbing his hair with pleasure.

"You're so wet for me," he said, tracing her center with his finger before plunging it into her. She moaned, unable to respond, and he worked with her. His finger plunged in and out while his tongue danced along her clit.

"Oh my god," she gasped, allowing her hips to rock into him. "You're going to make me cum." She felt her body tightening in pleasure.

"Good, I want you to cum on my fingers, before you cum on my dick." Moving his fingers faster. A scream broke from her mouth, and a wave of pleasure washed over her muscles, tightening one last time before releasing. "Good girl," he growled, stepping back and pulling down his shorts. His erection stood tall and proud. She felt her eyes widen as his rippled naked body stood before her.

"Condom, I have a condom in the top of my bag." She gasped, her toes curling, and muscles clenching again. He retrieved the condom quietly and slowly opened the package, rolling it onto himself. She groaned again. The anticipation sent ripples of pleasure through her. "I need you inside of me." Those words seemed to break his slow, steady movements. Like an animal, he pounced toward her, their lips colliding. The tip of his penis danced around her hole. She stroked his penis and gave his balls a light squeeze. He groaned into her mouth, and she guided his penis inside her. They both gasped. "You feel amazing," she moaned.

"That's my line," he whispered, returning his lips to her neck, and he slid his penis out and then slowly back in. "I don't know how long I can go, you feel so good." He slammed into her again.

"Faster," she commanded, wrapping her legs around his waist and entwining her fingers into his hair. He obeyed, picking up his pace. Indie felt like they moved in sync until both their bodies began to tense up. "I'm so close," she whispered into his neck. He slammed into her fast and hard. She felt her body begin to seize, and then, with a scream, waves of ecstasy washed over her. Somehow, he managed to move faster until his body shuddered with release, and he stopped moving, hovering over her.

"You are perfect," he whispered.

"You too," she responded and thought. "I think I'm falling in love with this man."

Sweet as Honey

NICOLE LINETTE

Chapter Thirty-Five

Indie collapsed onto her narrow bed inside her trailer, limbs still humming with leftover energy she didn't know what to do with. She stared up at the string lights twinkling above her head and let out a little laugh that sounded too dreamy, even to her own ears.

She reached for her phone, thumb hovering before typing a message to Sloane.

> I have so much to tell you, I don't even know where to start.

She hit send, then chewed her lip. A moment later, another thought spilled out.

> My heart is either going to burst or combust. Possibly both.

The three dots appeared instantly.

> Combustion means you finally got laid, doesn't it?

Indie slapped a hand over her face, groaning, but a laugh bubbled out anyway. She typed back quickly.

> Let's just say the beekeeper knows his way around more than hives.

Another bubble.

> I KNEW IT. Spill everything later. I want details—alll the sticky ones.

> I'm coming over like right now.

Indie squealed, tossing the phone onto the blanket beside her, but the grin on her face wouldn't quit. Her chest buzzed with the strange, giddy knowing that this wasn't just a fling.

It was something bigger, scarier, and sweeter than she'd ever planned on. She held the journal that Lucas had given her above her head; it felt like him. She clutched it to her chest.

"Oh, Bambi, I feel fantastic." She turned her head to look into Bambi's terrarium, surprised by the little tarantula's face looking back at her. "Oh, hey girl, good to see you moving around this lovely afternoon. We have a new friend coming over."

Sloane flung the door open, startling Indie out of her light sleep. "Girl, I'm so proud of you!" Sloane strolled in and flopped down on the bed next to Indie. Indie laughed and moved to sit beside her.

"What is that?" Sloane shrieked, pointing at Bambi.

Indie snorted.

"That's Bambi, she is my tarantula."

"Oh, that's right, I don't know why, but when you told me I was not picturing... her?"

"Do you want to hold her?" Indie asked.

"God no!"

Indie smiled at her friend. "Come on, let's get a fire going outside, and I will tell you everything."

The fire was crackling, and they sat curled up in blankets side by side in the hammocks, legs hanging over the edge, swaying.

"My first kiss was in middle school in the cafeteria line. It was grilled cheese day, and I can still remember the smell." Sloane closed her eyes, inhaling deeply. "All I truly wanted was my grilled cheese, but my boyfriend at the time, Shawn, Shane? I can't remember, he just stood there staring at me; then he leaned in and bam planted his lips on mine, it was weird. Then we both got detention for 'PDA' at school." She laughed, using a quotation finger as she said PDA. "My parents were so upset, pretty sure they sprouted grey hair as the principal was talking to them." Sloane started to laugh. Indie joined in laughter and comfort, feeling every inch for her.

"I am surprised you didn't smack the poor boy for standing between you and what you wanted." Indie gasped, catching her breath.

"I was tempted," Sloane responded before taking a sip of her cider. "Okay, your turn." She motioned for Indie to share her story.

"My first kiss was as an adult. I was at some dive bar in San Diego. Nothing too crazy. This guy swore I was the one after sharing a few drinks together. I gave him my number and never heard from him again. It was a funny memory, though."

"Wait... You didn't kiss anyone until you were an adult?!?" Sloane said, surprised.

"Yeah, I had no interest in boys at the time. I was just trying… to… you know," she waved her hand, "figure out my place," Indie responded more quietly, feeling as if she might have ruined the playful moment.

"I get that, and honestly, girl, you weren't missing much, boys were gross, I mean men are too most of the time." She shoulder bumped Indie, giving her an encouraging look. "Enough small talk, though. Tell me all about Lucas. Did his abs have like baby abs?" This comment got another laugh from Indie, reviving the playful moment.

The rest of the afternoon faded in a blur of conversation and laughter. Sloane swore she could sense how big Lucas's dick was just by his presence, and she waved her hands about to emphasize the size. Hot tea almost shot out of Indie's nose.

Later that evening, as Indie shuffled and sorted her inventory, Lucas pulled his truck into her campsite. She stood to greet him. "Want to come on a secret adventure?" Lucas asked, walking towards her. She instinctively held her arms out for an embrace. He pulled her tight to his chest. "Is it crazy that it's only been a couple of hours and I missed you?" he whispered.

Indie lay her head on his chest. "No." She pulled back, smoothing out her shirt, and she could feel a blush heating her face. "Also a secret adventure?" She arched an eyebrow.

He smirked, pulling away and motioning to the truck. "Sort of."

They drove in companionable silence, the road winding through golden fields. The air buzzed faintly with the sound of bees. Indie watched the landscape outside morph and change, dancing with the setting sun.

Lucas pulled over in a dense forested area. "This is toward the back of our property," he noted before climbing out and rushing to her door. Indie let out a laugh as Lucas opened the door to help her out of the truck. He led her down a narrow path until a cluster of hives came into view, tucked under the dappled shade of tall trees. Unlike the neat rows she'd seen before, this spot felt hidden, almost sacred.

Indie's eyes widened. "This feels like a fairytale spot."

Lucas nodded. "This is our oldest hive. We sort of let it manage itself, more of a bee-centric or holistic approach." He went to the back of the truck grabbing a beekeeping suit for her. "For your first time getting honey, I figured it would be best." He helped her climb into the suit and place the veil on her. Indie felt excitement at this new activity.

Her heart squeezed. She followed slowly behind him, watching him move with quiet reverence as he lifted the lid, the air filling with the earthy-sweet scent of honeycomb. He looked over his shoulder at her and gave her a nod to come closer.

For a moment, his gaze caught hers, something warm and unspoken flickering there, before he gently guided her hand toward the comb. She stifled a laugh as she watched a bee crawl up Lucas's sun-kissed skin, a stark contrast to her bright white gloves.

"I want to feel them," she whispered, unsure how noise affected bees. He nodded and slowly pulled her glove off. The bees crawled on her hands, and she was surprised at the warmth their tiny bodies emitted. Their little legs tickled faintly like being brushed with a feather. It reminds her of Bambi.

They worked side by side, bottling a small jar of honey together. Indie's fingers brushed his when she screwed on the lid, and she swore the air between them hummed louder than the bees.

Indie smiled and rocked with the music in the truck as she clutched her jar of honey. "You're right, that was a great secret adventure." She hummed, looking out the window, trying to pinpoint where they were in relation to his house.

"I thought so, but truly I had an ulterior motive." Lucas glanced at her with a smile.

"Oh? Are you trying to get me into bed again?" she responded by giving him a wink and watching his face flush slightly.

"Always," he said quickly, then cleared his throat. "I got a new terrarium for Randy, actually, and I wanted you to help me set it up. It got delivered to Charlotte's, though, so we need to pick it up."

"Oh, I'd love to see Charlotte and Olivia," Indie responded, realizing she had grown attached to the two even though their interactions had been limited.

Chapter Thirty-Six

Lucas

Lucas pulled into Charlotte's driveway, relieved to see Daniel's truck was gone. He led them into the house without knocking.

"Hey, Charlotte, Olivia," he called, opening the door and hearing a fuss in the kitchen. "Just stopping in for my package, Indie's here." He motioned for Indie to lead the way down the hall towards the kitchen.

"Oh, great, send her in," Charlotte called. Olivia sat at the table, markers scattered everywhere, working on a school project about pollinators.

"Indie," Charlotte said, holding a mixing bowl. "You're crafty, do you mind helping Olivia with the display while I finish this cake?" Lucas tilted his head.

"Why are you making a cake?" He watched Indie's smile grow as she slid into the chair next to Olivia.

"Show me what you've got," Indie said, glancing at him. Joy sparkling in her eyes.

Lucas lingered in the doorway, watching silently as Indie leaned close to Olivia. He watched them cut out bright construction-paper flowers and glued them onto a poster. Olivia chattered nonstop about bees, parroting facts Lucas had taught her, while Indie listened with genuine interest. He didn't realize that he forgot to listen to Charlotte's response until he felt her gaze staring at him. Charlotte's smile was unhindered and her eyes seemed to be screaming at him that she knew what he felt in his heart for Indie.

"Sorry, what was the cake for?" he asked, keeping his sister's gaze.

"One of Daniel's friends." She shrugged. "They are going out tonight and he wanted to take him a cake." Lucas could almost hear the suspicion in her voice. "I thought it was a lovely idea and that means Olivia and I can have mommy and daughter time," she chirped with a little too much excitement for his taste. He needs to make sure to set aside time to talk to Charlotte alone.

"Mommy and Me time," Olivia shouted from her spot at the table, knocking over the cup of water. Indie moved quickly to rescue the display. Before he could move to help, Charlotte was at the table dabbling the water with a cloth. The three girls around the dining table smiling with Indie holding the display up like a trophy would forever be an image that burned into his mind.

After the mess had been cleaned and Lucas managed to pry Olivia from Indie, he grabbed his package and they were off to his house. Indie sat strangely quiet, her jar of honey between her legs and her finger fidgeting with the lid. He felt as though she had something to say, panic washed over him. Maybe it was too much, spending this much time with him made her uncomfortable, and she was planning to leave without him. He turned into his driveway, his throat tightening as he searched for words, but her words broke first.

NICOLE LINETTE

Chapter Thirty-Seven

"**S**o... I've been thinking," she started, then faltered. Her throat tightened. What if he said no? What if this was just a beautiful week for him and nothing more? She shifted around on the seat turning towards him, he left the truck running. Maybe she should have done this at her campsite, so she could have run inside and locked herself in the trailer if things went bad.

Lucas turned to her, brows raised patiently, he looked concerned. "Thinking what?"

Indie sucked in a breath, counting down from three. She was just going to blurt it out. "What if you came with me? Like... really came with me. My next stop is Savannah. Or somewhere else. Doesn't matter. Just... with me." She heard her heartbeat in her ears.

The silence stretched long enough for her palms to go clammy. She was about to make a joke or take it back when she felt his finger lift her chin. She hadn't noticed that she was staring at the jar of honey, and her hands were clasping the necklace he'd given her.

Lucas tilted her head, so their gaze met, and his face seemed to relax. "You'd want me to come with you? For more than a few days?"

"Yes." Her voice cracked. "More than a few days."

A slow smile spread across his face, soft but certain. "I'd need some time to tell my family. Tie up loose ends with the farm. Maybe a month?" His voice was soft.

Relief flooded her so fast her eyes burned. "A month. Perfect. I'll be here. And then... we'll go."

He reached over, taking her restless hand in his. "Guess I'd better get used to driving that van of yours."

Indie laughed through the sting in her eyes, her whole body feeling lighter than it had in years. She slid closer to him, grabbing the back of his head and bringing it down for a kiss. This kiss felt different; it felt binding, like she had confirmation that he wanted her around, for at least a while longer.

That night, lying in bed, she picked up her phone again and typed one last message to Sloane.

Sloane's reply came instantly.

> Indie. Are you about to domesticate a farmer??

> Is it domestication if you're removing him from the farm?

> Wait, you can take the boy out of the farm, but you can't take the farm out of the boy.

Indie pressed the phone to her chest and let out a giddy laugh. For the first time in forever, she let herself believe she didn't have to keep moving alone.

> Wait wait, go... where?

NICOLE LINETTE

Chapter Thirty-Eight

Lucas

Lucas lay awake long after the farm had gone still, the night sounds drifting in through the open window. Crickets sang, a breeze rustled the trees, and somewhere in the distance one of the hives thrummed faintly. Normally, those sounds grounded him. Tonight, they felt like questions.

His hand still remembered the weight of Indie's smaller one in his, the way her thumb had twitched nervously against his skin, the way her voice quivered when she asked him to travel with her. The words had been shaky, but the hope behind them had been steady as bedrock.

He rolled onto his back, staring at the ceiling. The farm was his life, his family's life. Every nail in the barn, every row of clover, every hive buzzing with bees had been built by years of sweat and care. Leaving, even for a little while, wasn't something he'd ever imagined.

He could see the disappointment on his father's face, his mother trying to be happy for him but still feeling hurt. How can he leave Charlotte and Olivia? Olivia was so young. Did he really want to miss out on watching her grow up? How would all of the work get done?

But then he thought of Indie's laugh in the kitchen with Oliva, the way she leaned close as if the girl's every word mattered. He thought of her eyes widening with wonder when he showed her the old hive, her trust in him as she held her hand steady among the bees.

And he thought of the light in her face when he said yes.

A slow exhale left his chest. Maybe he didn't have to choose between the farm and this wild, reckless chance with her. Maybe, for once, he could loosen his grip on duty long enough to see what else life had to offer.

He closed his eyes, letting the picture form: Indie in the passenger seat of that lavender van, wind in her hair, him behind the wheel. For the first time in years, the thought of leaving didn't feel like running away. It felt like moving forward.

Roots & Wings

NICOLE LINETTE

Chapter Thirty-Nine

Lucas

The gravel crunched under his boots as Lucas pulled into the farmhouse drive. The familiar weight of home pressed down on his chest, only now it carried a sharp edge of nerves. He'd rehearsed the words a hundred times on the ride back, but every version ended with that look on his father's face.

Inside, the whole family was gathered. His mom was at the stove, Charlotte was leaning against the counter with Olivia perched on it, and Hank was at the table flipping through the newspaper. It smelled like coffee and fresh bread, homey in a way Lucas suddenly realized he was about to leave behind. He was relieved not to see Daniel in the kitchen, but that relief dissipated when he heard a truck pulling in. Suddenly, he felt rushed, so he stepped further into the kitchen.

He cleared his throat. "I need to tell you all something."

Josephine turned first, a smile already waiting. "You look nervous, honey. Spit it out."

He rubbed the back of his neck. "I've decided to travel with Indie. Just for a while. We leave in a month. So I can get things in order here, then I'll go with her to Savannah. Maybe longer. I thought with all the new help and machines, maybe you could be fine without me for a while?" He felt like he was rambling, like the conversation he overheard when he was younger, and all the feelings were starting to swell inside him.

The room shifted.

His dad's paper rustled sharply. Hank lowered it, brows drawn. "Travel? With the girl in the van?"

Lucas's jaw tightened, but before he could answer, his mother stepped forward, eyes shining. She clasped his face in both hands like she'd been waiting years for this moment. "Oh, Lucas. I knew it the minute I saw you two together. She's the one, isn't she? My sweet little bumble finally found his person."

Heat crept up his neck.

Beaming and tears brimming in her eyes. "You go see the world, sweetheart. The farm will be here when you get back."

Hank scoffed. "The world doesn't need to be seen." His father's brow crinkled. Lucas knew his family meant everything to his father even more than the farm.

Josephine swatted his arm with a dish towel. "Oh, for heaven's sake, Hank. Let the boy breathe. You'll give him gray hair before he even leaves."

Charlotte laughed, clapping her hands together. "Finally! My brother is in love. I'm already planning the goodbye party. You're not getting out of that, by the way. And promise me every Christmas, no matter where you are, you're back here with us."

Lucas chuckled softly. "Deal."

It was then he noticed Olivia, quiet in the corner, her little shoulders shaking. His heart twisted. He crouched down, lifting her gently into his arms.

"Hey, what's all this, bug?"

Her voice came out in a whisper, broken. "You're leaving."

Lucas kissed her damp cheek, holding her tight. "I'll always come back. Always. And maybe, if your mom and dad say yes, you can come with me sometimes. Think you'd like to ride in Indie's van?"

Olivia sniffled, nodding against his shoulder.

"Then we'll make it happen. But before I go, you and I have a special day coming. Just us. Deal?"

She pulled back enough to meet his eyes and gave a watery smile. "Deal."

Just then, the door in the living room swung open, and Daniel strolled inside. "What's going on?" he called, closing the distance to the kitchen quickly.

"Lucas is gonna travel with Indie." Olivia sniffled, squeezing Lucas. Lucas met Daniel's eyes; he could have sworn something shifted in them, but he couldn't figure out what.

Chapter Forty

Indie sprawled across Sloane's studio floor, a half-finished embroidery hoop in her lap while Sloane scrolled on her phone nearby.

"So you're really doing it?" Sloane asked, voice tight. "Leaving me for some farmer with nice arms and bees?"

Indie grinned, threading her needle. "Nice arms, yes. Bees, yes. And also, maybe... love."

Sloane groaned dramatically, flopping back on the rug. "Love. Gross. What am I supposed to do without you? You're my partner."

Indie set the hoop down, softer now. "You'll be fine. Better than fine. You've got yoga, Butterscotch, your whole weird, wonderful life here."

Sloane sat up suddenly, snapping her fingers. "Okay, I'm not gonna mope. I'm going to make you help me with goat yoga before you leave." She paused. "Like you promised." She narrowed her eyes playfully.

Indie laughed, clapping. "Yes! Of course."

"And," Sloane added, handing her a scrap of fabric, "before you run off with Mr. Honey Hands, you owe me one last project. Embroider my cat. I need him immortalized. On a pillow. Or maybe a tote bag."

Indie rolled her eyes but smiled, already sketching. "Done, but only because your cat looks like he's plotting world domination, and I feel the world should know."

They dissolved into laughter, but under it lingered a tender weight, the ache of goodbye, and the hope that distance wouldn't dim what they had.

Chapter Forty-One

True to his word, Lucas set aside the next morning for Olivia. She bounded out of the house with her backpack already stuffed, eyes still a little red but glowing with excitement.

"Where are we going?" she asked as he lifted her into the truck.

He winked. "Secret adventure. You'll see."

They drove down winding back roads until they reached the edge of a quiet meadow, one of Lucas's favorite places to sit when he needed to think. Wildflowers stretched in every direction, bees humming lazily from bloom to bloom.

Olivia's gasp made his chest tighten in the best way. "It looks like a fairyland."

Lucas laid out a blanket, pulling a small basket from the truck's bed. Inside were peanut butter and jelly sandwiches cut into hearts, honey cookies he'd baked that morning, and two mason jars of lemonade. Olivia squealed like it was Christmas.

They ate, crumbs scattering across the blanket, while Lucas told her stories about the bees. How they always found their way home, no matter how far they traveled. Olivia listened with wide eyes, her sticky fingers clutching a cookie.

"So if you go far away with Indie," she asked softly, "you'll still be like the bees? You'll come home?"

Lucas swallowed hard and nodded, brushing a curl from her forehead. "Exactly like the bees. No matter how far I go, I'll always find my way back here. Back to you."

She leaned into his side, small and warm against him, and he wrapped an arm around her shoulders.

After they finish their picnic, they spend the afternoon catching grasshoppers, making flower crowns, and lying back in the grass to watch clouds drift by. Olivia declared it the best day ever, and Lucas silently promised himself he'd create more of these memories.

When the sun dipped low and fireflies began blinking in the tall grass, Lucas packed them up and drove home, Olivia dozing against his arm with a flower crown tilted on her head.

He looked at her and thought, not for the first time, that love didn't just tie him here. It could also be the thing that gave him the courage to leave, knowing he had something worth coming back to.

How was your day with Olivia?

It was like a fairy wonderland adventure.

Your words or hers?

Both of ours, I'm a prince, didn't you know?

My prince in shining armor.

Want to come over?

Already headed there.

NICOLE LINETTE

Chapter Forty-Two

Indie

Indie was sitting on Lucas's front step, sketchbook balanced on her knees, when she heard the crunch of tires on gravel. She looked up just as Lucas's truck rolled in, dust curling around it in the golden light of dusk.

Olivia tumbled sleepily out of the cab, a crooked flower crown still clinging to her curls, and Lucas scooped her easily into his arms. He whispered something that made the girl giggle before resting her head against his shoulder again.

Indie's chest tightened at the sight of him with Olivia, steady and gentle, carrying love and responsibility so naturally it made her heart ache. This was more than a man chasing adventure with her. This was a man rooted deep in his people, and still brave enough to step into something new.

Lucas caught her watching and offered a small smile, the kind that said he didn't need words to share the moment.

Indie lifted her sketchbook, tapping the pencil against the page. "Flower crowns suit you, farmer."

He chuckled softly, adjusting Olivia in his arms. "Careful, or I'll have you out here making one tomorrow."

She grinned, warmth blooming in her chest. "Don't tempt me with a good time," she called as he carried Olivia inside.

Indie lingered on the step a moment longer, watching the door swing shut behind them. The fireflies had started their evening dance in the tall grass, their faint glow blinking like tiny lanterns. She closed her sketchbook, hugging it to her chest before slipping inside.

The house was hushed except for the soft creak of floorboards upstairs. She wandered toward the living room, her gaze catching on the shelves lined with framed photos and well-worn books. One frame stood out as a black and white wedding photo, edges slightly faded, of two young faces brimming with certainty.

Lucas came down a few minutes later, his steps quieter now that Olivia was tucked in. He noticed her standing there and followed her gaze.

"My parents," he said simply, moving to stand beside her. "They got married when they were 18. Everyone thought it wouldn't last. Too young, too hard, too much stacked against them."

Indie glanced up at him, curiosity softening her features. "And yet?"

"And yet, they're still together. Fifty years come spring." His mouth curved, but there was a weight to it. "They fight, they drive each other crazy sometimes, but they never quit. To them, marriage isn't something you walk away from. It's a promise you keep."

The truth of his words settled into her bones. She studied the photo again, the way his mother leaned into his father as if there was no storm strong enough to shake them apart.

"That kind of love," she murmured, almost to herself, "feels rare these days."

Lucas's eyes found hers, steady and unflinching. "It's the only kind I believe in."

The room seemed to still be around them, the hum of the summer night pressing close through the open window. Indie swallowed, heat rising in her cheeks under the weight of his gaze. For a moment, the air was thick with things neither of them dared to say.

Then Lucas cleared his throat, breaking the spell with a quiet smile. "You hungry? I can make us something before it gets too late."

Indie returned his smile, though her heart was still caught on his words, beating a little too fast. "Only if you promise to wear a flower crown while you cook."

He chuckled, shaking his head as he moved toward the kitchen. "Don't push your luck, market girl."

Indie couldn't stop herself from glancing back at the photo one last time, a seed of longing rooting itself deep inside her.

She trailed behind Lucas as they moved to the kitchen. "Grilled cheese and soup?" he asked, glancing over his shoulder.

"That sounds great," she responded, taking in the small kitchen. The kitchen was surprisingly modern compared to the rustic, country appearance of the rest of the house.

"Yeah, I know it looks a little different from the rest of the house, but it spoke to me." He laughed, noticing her surprise. He motioned to the barstool at the breakfast bar.

The seat from the barstool left her staring at Lucas's back as he started to shred cheese, the smell of the fresh tomato soup filling the kitchen.

"So, tell me about Daniel and Charlotte. How did they meet? How is their relationship?"

Lucas took a deep breath. Indie could feel the distaste radiating from Lucas.

"There always seems to be something off with them. I used to think they had a great relationship until I looked closer. It feels like a facade. Well, on Charlotte's part. Daniel always seems angry and uninterested. They got together in high school, he just rolled in his senior year like he owned the place, and by that spring he had Charlotte."

"Oh... that's unfortunate, so she never dated anyone else?"

"Just Daniel, as far as I know. I'm not sure why she stays with him; they don't seem happy together at all," Lucas said, sagging his shoulders, as he placed the sandwiches in the pan.

"Maybe she believes marriage is forever, like your parents, and is afraid to be a failure. She holds on and tries to make everyone believe everything is perfect." The wonder escaped her mouth before she had time to think about it. Her own words made her flinch, and she watched for his reaction.

Lucas turned his face, set in a grown, but realization seemed to shine in his eyes. She clenched her jaw with anticipation. "I never thought of that. That's a good perspective, maybe I should find some way to tell her it's okay." His brows knitted together. "Thank you," he said, giving her a small smile, allowing her to relax her muscles. She gave him a smile as he turned his attention back to the sandwiches.

"You're a good brother."

"Sometimes." He laughed, flipping a sandwich.

Storm of Reckoning

NICOLE LINETTE

Chapter Forty-Three

Lucas

The rain pounded against the truck roof; it had poured down on his way back from town and was just now lightning up. He turned down the gravel drive just in time to see Daniel's taillights disappearing around the bend. Lucas lifted a hand automatically in his usual wave, not knowing that the wave marked the last normal moment before everything changed.

He spotted Olivia in the field and pulled the truck over outside Charlotte's. "Bug?" he called out to her, but she didn't respond or move; fear pulsed through him. He quickly closed the gap between him and her. Olivia was kneeling in the grass, her clothes damp, and Otis was standing grazing on the grass beside her. She clutched a fistful of wildflowers, her cheeks streaked with tears. Lucas's chest tightened.

"Hey, bug. What's going on?" His first thought was that she was thinking about him leaving again.

She sniffled, wiping her nose with the back of her hand. "Daddy's leaving."

Lucas frowned. "I know. He'll be back soon. Probably just had to run an errand." He knelt down before her his arms out for a hug.

But Olivia shook her head, her voice breaking. "No. I heard them. He told Mommy he never wants to see us again. He packed his bags. He's gone. Mommy's crying."

The words hit Lucas like a gut punch. He swallowed hard, rage already clawing at his ribs. He forced his tone steady. "Your mom was crying?"

Olivia nodded, a fresh tear sliding down her cheek.

Lucas pulled her into his arms, hugging her tightly. He stood up holding her tightly against him. He fired a text off to Indie.

Need backup. Can you take Olivia for a bit?

Indie's reply came quickly.

On my way.

Lucas set Olivia in the truck wrapping his jacket around her. "Okay, bug, you stay here. I'm gonna check on your mom." He left the door open and took the keys.

Inside, the house felt heavy, quiet, except for the sound of muffled sobs. Lucas paused in the hallway, pinpointing the sound. Charlotte's door was cracked just enough for him to see her, crumpled on the floor, sobbing into her hands. He took a breath, then pushed the door open.

"Char," he whispered.

She didn't look up. Lucas crossed the room, kneeling down, and without a word, he wrapped his arms around her. She collapsed against him, shaking, grief pouring out in waves.

He held her, trying to be steady and solid, his shirt damp with tears. When her sobs finally slowed, he carefully picked her up and carried her to the bed. He helped her climb under the blankets trying to get a look at her face, but she turned away from him.

"I'll be right back."

He went back outside as Indie's purple van pulled into the driveway. He gave her a wave and went to the truck.

Olivia was curled in his jacket lying in a ball on his seat.

"Come here, bug." He leaned in and scooped her up. "Indie is here and she's going to take you to go meet Bambi."

Olivia sniffled in his arms but didn't respond. He felt his heart breaking. He pulled her in close, resting his chin on her head.

Indie had parked and was walking over.

"Can you take Olivia to your campsite?" he asked.

Indie nodded, giving him a questioning look.

"I'll fill you in later," he said, leading the way to Indie's van.

She opened the back door for him. He set Olivia in and buckled her up.

He held his arms out for Indie, giving her a quick hug and a kiss on the forehead. "Thank you."

He handed her the bag with the change of clothes. "I'll talk to you soon."

Indie nodded, stepping back from him, giving her a view of Olivia.

"You know, I think some ice cream sounds yummy, and then maybe some cocoa by the campfire?" Her voice was soft, and he could see Olivia coming back into her body, and he, too, felt a bit better.

"I'll see my two best girls very soon," he said before planting another kiss on Indie's head and going back inside.

He entered Charlotte's bedroom. Charlotte hadn't moved; her sobs still filled the room. He passed by her and went into the bathroom to run a bath. He set a towel and a robe nearby. He remembered she loved baths. In fact, she and Daniel had a whole fight about putting such a big bath in the main bathroom when they built the house. He shook the memory away. The more he thought of Daniel, the more the pain for his sister and niece became rage.

He went over to the bed and knelt down, speaking softly. "Hey, Charlotte, let's get you in the bath, okay?" He paused for a moment. Maybe he should call his mom, but he felt like Charlotte wouldn't want that. Charlotte groaned.

"Lucas, I just don't understand." Her tears came faster. He pulled her to him.

"I know, I don't either." He hugged her, tears filling his own eyes. He'd never seen her in so much pain, not even when she fell from the loft and broke her leg.

"He's gone, he doesn't want us, what did I do wrong?" she wailed. Lucas squeezed tighter.

"It has nothing to do with you; he's trash, he doesn't deserve you."

"I love him. He's not trash! I love him." She pushed back from him suddenly, her grief washing away to anger on her face. "You never liked him, but I loved him; he wouldn't have just left if I didn't do anything."

"Char..."

"You don't understand, Lucas, you don't understand." Her voice rose, and she scurried across the bed, her eyes wide and crazed like a scared animal. "Just go, just go," she yelled, pressing her back against the wall and sinking to the ground.

Lucas backed out of the room. "We have Olivia," he called, his voice sounding shaky to his own ears. The only response was a wailing sound from Charlotte. He went to Olivia's room, quickly packing her a bag before giving his mom a call.

He got into his truck. Daniel had done this. And Lucas wasn't going to let him walk away without consequences.

Memories of Daniel disregarding Charlotte's feelings floating through Lucas's mind. All the times he showed everyone how much he did not care about Charlotte or anyone in their family or town.

Daniel's blank stare, his nitpicky comments, the way there was no love or softness towards Charlotte or Olivia. It all started to burn in his mind, how could he have let this go on for so long? The guilt punched him in the stomach, he should have protected his family sooner. He reassured himself that he could make amends for his delay now, and that was just what he was planning to do.

Chapter Forty-Four

Indie

Indie pulled the van over outside the ice cream shop and looked back at Olivia. The girl's cheeks were puffy, but she smiled faintly at Indie.

"Ice cream?" Indie asked softly. Olivia nodded. Indie went around and opened the door, grabbing Olivia's cold little hand.

They wandered into town, cones in hand. They strolled along the shops, stopping to peer in windows. It was a softer silence than the car ride, as if the ice cream had brought Olivia's energy up just a little.

"Let's stop at this bench for a little bit and finish our cones." Indie motioned to the bench, giving them a good view of the bay. Olivia sat down and watched her closely.

"Where's your mom and dad?" Olivia asked, returning her gaze to the cone. Indie glanced at her and then out over the bay.

"Well..." she hummed, trying to think of a response.

"Are you gonna lie to me?" Olivia's words caught her off guard.

"Wh-What." She turned her body to face her.

"Grown-ups sometimes lie to me," she whispered as if it were a secret. "Sometimes I know what they say is a lie."

Indie exhaled.

"No, I'm not going to lie to you. It's just hard. My mom died when I was little, and I still miss her."

"Do you still cry?" Indie nodded, giving her a small smile.

"Yeah, sometimes, it's gotten a little easier with all these new wonderful people I'm meeting." She reached down and squeezed Olivia's sticky hand.

"What about your dad?"

"That's a little harder, I never met my dad. He didn't really want a baby, so he left." She studied Olivia's face, looking for any signs that she would burst into tears again.

"My dad didn't want me either," she replied so low that Indie had to lean forward.

"I don't know about that, sometimes grown-ups make poor choices, but he had love for you."

"No, I don't think so." She swung her legs back and forth and picked at a string on her shirt. Indie felt her heart breaking, she understood the pain of not having an active father figure. "Lucas likes me."

"Honey, Lucas loves you. I don't think he loves anyone more than he loves you."

"I think he loves you too," she said looking up and making eye contact with Indie. "I think it's okay if he goes away for a little bit." Her eyes started to well up with tears. Indie watched the last of the ice cream drip from the bottom of Olivia's cone. "'Cause he promised he'd come back one day." Her little voice shook, and a tear slid down her face. Indie scooped the girl into her arms, causing both cones to fall to the ground.

"Oh, honey, he won't ever stay away from you. Lucas will never leave you." Indie knew with all her heart that Olivia needed Lucas, and in some way, it healed the little girl inside her, but in another way, it shattered the woman she was.

NICOLE LINETTE

Chapter Forty-Five

Lucas

By nightfall, the storm picked back up. Rain hammered the truck roof, matching the pounding in Lucas's chest. His knuckles whitened against the steering wheel as he pulled into the parking lot of a dive bar just outside town.

Neon lights buzzed above the drop, flickering like they wanted to escape their own cage. Lucas sat for a long second, blood boiling, replaying Charlotte's sobs, Olivia's trembling voice. His skin prickled with rage.

He reached for the door handle and then his phone buzzed.

A text from Indie.

> I definitely ship our tarantulas, Ram-Bam.

Attached was a picture of her embroidery hoop: two small tarantulas, holding legs, a heart above them. Then a picture of Olivia snuggled into blankets in her hammock.

Lucas's breath hitched. For a heartbeat, the fury cracked, replaced by something fragile and good. But then the door to the bar opened, and the music brought his anger back.

He tucked the phone away, jaw tightening, and climbed from the truck.

Music slammed into him the second he pushed through the door.

Heads turned when he stormed toward the corner, eyes locked on Daniel. A woman who looked slightly familiar sat on his lap, and in front of them was the cake Charlotte made, half eaten, with two forks stabbed into the middle like a cruel representation of what Daniel had done to Charlotte's heart.

Daniel was smiling, waving down the bartender, an empty glass at his elbow. He turned just as Lucas reached him.

In one swift motion, Lucas seized his shirt collar and slammed him against the wall. Glasses shattered. Voices dropped to a hush.

"Lucas," Daniel choked, fingers tightening around Lucas's wrists.

Lucas's voice was low, dangerous. "How could you?"

Something ugly sparked in Daniel's eyes. "You don't understand. You'll never understand."

Lucas yanked him closer, the roar of the bar fading to a muffled hum.

Daniel shoved back, spitting the words like venom. "We aren't even married. I never filed the papers. I didn't want this. I don't want to play house on your farm. I don't want tea parties and dress-up. This isn't me."

The world froze around Lucas's ribs. Six years. For six years, his sister had built a life on a promise Daniel never intended to keep.

"You think you're better than me?" Daniel rasped, lip curling. "I'm not the only one running from this life."

Lucas slammed him into the wall again, rage shaking through every muscle. "You don't get to walk away from them. Not Charlotte. Not Olivia."

Daniel smirked. "Then stop me."

Daniel dropped his weight suddenly, ripping free of Lucas's grip. Then he drove forward like a linebacker, and the two of them crashed through a table. Beer geysered, wood splintered, and the bar erupted into chaos.

Lucas's knuckles burned. Blood leaked from the split in his brow. Daniel was on top of him, ready to swing, but before it made contact, Lucas rolled, pinning him to the floor, his forearm pushing into Daniel's neck. Daniel writhed beneath him, teeth bared, laughing through the pain.

"You'll never keep her happy, Lucas! Just like I couldn't. This place eats you alive."

Lucas felt a growl rising as he drew his arm back, ready to punch Daniel. Glass bit into his skin through his jeans, fury pulsing through him. The crowd pressed in—half-silent, half-roaring. One more second and he'd cross a line he couldn't take back.

Then a voice cut through everything.

"Lucas."

Not loud, but steady. Unyielding.

Lucas froze, breath jagged. He didn't need to look to know. Hank.

The crowd shifted as the older man stepped forward, weathered face unreadable in the dim bar lights.

"Get up, son."

Lucas's hands trembled, his first still raised above Daniel. "He's—"

"I said, get up." Hank's tone cracked like a whip.

Slowly, Lucas pushed off and rose, chest still tight with rage. Daniel lay sprawled on the floor, coughing, smirking through his busted lip.

Hank's gaze dropped to him, cold and sharp. "If a man's already out the door," he said, voice carrying over the crowd, "there ain't no fight in the world that's gonna make him stay. All you'll do is bleed yourself dry trying."

The words hit harder than any punch. Lucas felt something in him buckle.

Daniel spat blood onto the floor, chuckling low. "Finally, someone gets it."

Lucas lunged again, only to feel Hank's hand clamp firmly on his arm.

"Enough," Hank said. His grip was steady, immovable. "Let him go, he isn't worth our time."

Lucas stood there, trembling, caught between rage and grief, staring down at the man who was tearing his family apart. His father gave him another tug, and Lucas's feet started to move towards the exit against his will. He felt dazed, like everything was moving too slowly. He stopped holding the door open when he no longer felt his father's presence. Lucas glanced back, seeing Hank standing over Daniel. Everything fell quiet as if Hank commanded the universe. Daniel's demeanor seemed to waver under Hank's gaze.

"I'm a patient man," Hank spoke in a calm, firm voice, "but I promise you, if you set foot on my land, or come near my family again, they will have to kill me to stop me from ripping you apart." The rain seemed to grow louder as if confirming Hank's statement. Hank turned and walked steadily towards Lucas. "Get in your truck and get out of my town," Hank called over his shoulder, breezing past Lucas. "Come on, son, we have things to take care of."

Feeling defeated and exhausted, Lucas followed his father outside. As he walked, he pulled his phone out to see if Charlotte had said anything in their family group chat.

> Hey, Charlotte, can I bring you anything?

> Olivia says she loves you.

> I'm worried about you.

> Honey, I'm coming in. Love Mom

> I'm here for you, my baby girl. Dad

Olive Branch

NICOLE LINETTE

Chapter Forty-Six

Indie laughed as Olivia attempted to jump the hopscotch they made on the park sidewalk. She had spent every afternoon with Olivia the past week as her family tended to the farm and Charlotte. She had learned a lot about the family in this time of chaos.

Hank was seriously protective; he had changed every lock on Charlotte's house and installed an alarm system. He moved one of his livestock dogs outside Charlotte's house. Indie wasn't sure what that would do, but she didn't question Hank.

Josephine had been making and freezing food, maybe out of anxiety because now everyone's fridges and freezers were stuffed. She had also been the only person Charlotte let into the house, and she probably scrubbed every inch of Daniel from the house. This made Indie's heart hurt; she wondered how Olivia would feel if all the pieces of her dad were suddenly gone. She would have to make sure to talk to Lucas about it.

Lucas had become diligent in his work and care for Olivia. He gave Indie money today to take Olivia on a shopping spree, and he had even installed a swing set at his house. Indie couldn't help but feel the love that poured in from everyone for Olivia.

"Come on, Olivia, why don't we go get our shopping started?" Indie called, breaking her own thoughts.

"Okay! I think I want a new dress!" Olivia yelled, running back to the bench and grabbing her backpack that Indie embroidered with images of Otis. Indie smiled and let Olivia lead the way.

They were outside the flower shop, and Olivia was inspecting the pots of succulents. "Hmm, these aren't right," Olivia murmured, moving to the next display. The florist walked out, setting down another vase of flowers.

"Are you looking for anything particular?" she asked, crouching down to Olivia's level.

"My mom needs a plant. I have a picture." Olivia flung her bag around and dug through it, pulling out a drawing. "She drew this. I think she wants it?" The florist looked at the image.

"Hmm, I think I has something similar inside, come on." She waved her hand towards the door. "Also, I love your goat bag. Does that goat have three legs?" Olivia jumped up with a big smile.

"Indie made it, it's my goat Otis, he has three legs, he lives in a house. I named him," Olivia chirped, wandering around inside with Indie following close behind.

"That's lovely, do you take custom orders?" She turned to Indie. "I have an old basset hound I'd love to see memorialized."

Indie blinked, surprised. "I... yes. I can."

Within minutes, Olivia had found her desired flower and walked out of the flower shop with the biggest smile she had all week. As they walked, Olivia was telling every passerby that Indie had put Otis on her bag and she could help them too. Indie's cheeks felt warm from the praise and admiration the town folks gave her as they walked.

Indie provided her business card to two other townsfolk, one asking about a handkerchief for her sister's wedding and another a table runner. At some point, Olivia spoke to anyone who would listen about "goat yoga," Sloane's business idea, drawing a laugh and interest from passersby.

Indie felt something bloom inside her she hadn't expected. A sense that maybe this little town saw her as more than a passing traveler.

She squeezed Olivia's hand. "You're a natural business partner, you know that?"

Olivia grinned, teeth sticky with ice cream. "I'll keep telling everyone about goat yoga and your creations! We'll be famous."

Indie laughed, her heart warming. It wasn't just about distracting Olivia anymore. It was about showing her there was still joy to be found, even in the middle of heartache.

Chapter Forty-Seven

Lucas

Nights were the hardest. Olivia loved her afternoons with Indie and even seemed happy at dinner with his parents, but as soon as it was time to tuck her into his spare room, the tears came. She didn't understand why Charlotte wouldn't just open the door for her, and he didn't know what to say. She missed her mom, and he's sure to some degree missed her dad, not that she had asked about him once in the past week.

"Lucas, I want to go home now." Olivia sniffled. Lucas was sitting in the chair next to her bed.

"I know, love bugs. Your mom misses you so very much, and I'm sure she is just making sure everything is perfect for you."

"I just want my mommy." She started to cry. Lucas leaned over, hugging her.

"I know," he whispered, "I want her too." He missed his sister. This couldn't go on for much longer; he had to find a way to bring Charlotte back to reality. She had a daughter who needed her. "You know tomorrow is goat yoga, I am sure that will be so much fun." He tried to give his best happy smile, hoping to distract her.

"Yeah, Indie said I have an important job, and she'll even pay me." Olivia sniffed in response, rubbing her nose with the back of her hand and pulling the blankets up higher. "I think Mom would have liked goat yoga, but I don't think she's going to come."

"Yeah, probably not to this one, but maybe we can hold a special one for her. For her and Grandma, like a private goat yoga session." He stood up, giving her a kiss on the forehead. "We all need our rest so we have energy for tomorrow," he responded, watching her close her eyes. Slowly, he backed out of the room, closing the door behind him.

You ready for goat yoga tomorrow?

Go-yort

Like a combination of goat yoga.

Too similar to Go-Gurt, try again.

Yo, Go Goat? How's Olivia tonight?

Same as last night.

That sounds like a scooter brand.

I'm sorry. I hope things get better soon. I hate this for Olivia and Charlotte.

I wish I was with you right now.

Kiss face, you'll see me soon enough.

NICOLE LINETTE

Goat Yoga & Honey Hearts

NICOLE LINETTE

Chapter Forty-Eight

The farmhouse was quiet in a way that wasn't peaceful. Commonly, Charlotte's laughter filled the kitchen or her footsteps padded down the hall, but now she stayed behind a closed bedroom door. The air felt heavier without her in it.

Lucas knocked once that morning, then again, but there was no answer. Finally, he pressed his forehead against the wood, whispering, "We'll be here when you're ready."

Olivia tugged on his hand. "Is Mommy sick? Or sad still?"

Lucas crouched, brushing a strand of hair from her face. "Maybe a little bit of both."

Her brow wrinkled the way Charlotte's did when she tried to unravel a puzzle. "Can I make her soup? Or maybe cookies? She likes those."

Lucas's chest ached, but he was glad the morning seemed to chase away last night's tears. "Yeah, maybe we can make some cookies later and drop them off. How about we get ready for goat yoga?"

He quickly added, "I know it's hard being away from your mom right now, but I promise this won't be forever. Your mom will be better soon. She just needs a little time."

Olivia turned towards him, biting her quivering lip. "You promise?"

Lucas felt the lump in his throat rise. "I do." He gave her a squeeze and a tickle until the moment of tension was broken by her laughter, then together they went to get ready for goat yoga.

By late morning, the pasture was alive with bleats and giggles. Sloane had shown up early, her car filled with mats and excitement in her eyes.

"You're a saint for letting me use your land, Lucas," she said as she spread mats across the grass. "People are dying for something new around here. Goat yoga is going to be huge."

Lucas smirked. "Well, if the goats don't eat your students' hair, maybe."

As if on cue, one of the younger goats hopped onto a yoga mat and started chewing on the corner. Olivia shrieked with laughter, chasing it down.

"I'm the goat boss today!" she declared, tying a ribbon around the goat's neck like a badge or honor.

Indie appeared then, carrying a basket with little hand-stitched bandanas, each embroidered with a tiny flower. "Thought your goats could use a wardrobe upgrade," she teased, slipping one over the goat's head.

Lucas's lips twitched into a smile he couldn't quite contain. "You spoil them."

"Please," Indie said, grinning. "They deserve spa day energy too. Also, yes, I have some sweat rags with your logo on them as well," she responded before Sloane could ask.

When Sloane's first students arrived, Olivia stood at the edge of the mats with hands on her hips, clearly taking her role as goat wrangler very seriously. Before class began, she marched up to Sloane and set something in her hands. A small jar of golden honey with a crooked little label.

"This is my payment," she said proudly. "For my yoga spot."

Sloane blinked, then burst out laughing. "Sweetheart, you don't have to pay to be here."

Olivia crossed her arms. "It's real, honey. Uncle Lucas made it. It's good enough."

Lucas's throat tightened, warmth flooding his chest. Indie caught his eye and mouthed, "She's yours, through and through."

Lucas wasn't sure why he was so surprised by the number of people that had shown up, but every mat was taken. The class itself was chaotic, in his opinion. Goats were climbing over anything they could, nudging people out of poses, Olivia trying to "teach" a goat to do downward dog, but it was the best kind of chaos. Laughter echoed across the field, bright and healing, chasing away the silence that had hung over the house all week.

He was intentionally not trying to stare at Indie, as her laughter seemed to be more alluring than anyone else. He was amazed at how she could bend and twist, and it ignited his desire to scoop her up and take her to his bed. He exhaled and returned his attention to making sure the water cooler had plenty of ice, while he set out samples of bread and honey.

Sloane, Indie, and Lucas sat on the last of the mats to be put away, sipping on congratulatory wine his mother brought them when the last of the participants left. The three had sat there reflecting.

"How's Char?" Sloane asked, gazing in the direction of Charlotte's house even though she couldn't see. Lucas shrugged.

"I'm not sure, she let our mom in, but no one else," he responded.

"I never liked him. Daniel, I don't know, in high school it all seemed a bit much." Sloane took another drink of her wine. Lucas's eyebrows pinched in, and Indie stared ahead, watching Olivia sprawled out in the grass as if she were napping.

"What do you mean?" Lucas never liked Daniel either, but he couldn't remember any incidents in high school.

"You know, he just wanted her to do what he wanted. I felt like she gave up things she wanted."

"Like what?" Indie asked, turning her attention to them.

"You know," Sloane waved her hand as if motioning to everything, "like cheerleading, she loved that, but he didn't want other people watching her. She also used to wear the cutest clothes." Lucas frowned; he remembered she dropped out of cheerleading. It was around the time she started dating Daniel.

"We sort of stopped hanging out once she went into high school. I figure it was just normal for siblings to do that." He looked from Sloane to Indie, they both, as far as he knew, were only children.

"She'll find her way it's just going to take time," Indie said, giving him a small smile.

NICOLE LINETTE

Chapter Forty-Nine

Indie

The sun was hanging in the sky, bringing in the late afternoon breeze. The goats had wandered back toward the barn, their little bandanas askew, and the conversation had turned to Sloane's ideas for the next class. She had practically been buzzing with ideas as she waved goodbye to them.

Indie lingered at the edge of the pasture, her hands brushing the top of tall grass. Lucas came up beside her, silent at first, watching Olivia chase fireflies in the last stretch of daylight.

"She's something else," Indie murmured, nodding toward Olivia.

Lucas followed her gaze. She could see his jaw working as if he were chewing words he wasn't sure how to say. He let out a breath, slow and heavy, running a hand over the back of his neck. "I didn't know how to fix it for Charlotte. I still don't. But then you show up with goat scarves and turn the whole damn field into a circus... and suddenly, it's easier to breathe."

Indie's chest tightened, warmth blooming where her nerves usually lived. She bumped her shoulder gently against his arm. "Well, for the record, your goats are naturals. Total yogis."

That earned her a chuckle, low and warm. He glanced down at her, his eyes catching the last of the sun. "Indie?"

"Mm?"

"Thanks. For showing up the way you do. For her. For Oliva. For me."

The words weren't grand, but they landed like something sacred. Indie swallowed, the weight of them pressing into her chest.

She smiled, a little shaky. "Anytime, farmer boy."

For a heartbeat, the world went quiet except for Olivia's laughter and the hum of crickets. Lucas's hand brushed her, hesitant, fleeting, but it was enough to make her pulse stutter.

Then Olivia came barreling toward them, breathless with excitement. "Lucas! A butterfly landed on me!"

The moment broke, but the warmth of it lingered, humming under Indie's skin like the glow of the sky all around them.

Girls, Guts, & Gilmore

NICOLE LINETTE

Chapter Fifty

Indie leaned against the side of her lavender bus, watching the bustle of the Saturday market unfold around her. The familiar hum of chatter, the salty tang of the sea air, and the scent of fried dough drifting from the nearby booth had begun to feel... dare she admit it? Like home.

"Morning, Indie," Mrs. Murphy from the bakery called, sliding an extra blueberry scone into a bag. "Extra one for you. Looks like you've had a long week."

Indie smiled, touched more than she expected by the act of kindness. It had been a busy Saturday, but her heart still hurt a little knowing the Carrington stand went unmanned. It was just an empty space that the other vendors seemed to respect. It was as if everyone in the town was hurting for Charlotte and Olivia.

"Thank you, Mrs. Murphy. How's your granddaughter doing with her braces?" Her words flowed with easy, as she gave him a soft small.

Mrs. Murphy's eyes lit with surprise and pride. "Oh, she's adjusting just fine. Sweet of you to remember." Mrs. Murphy had loved goat yoga; she had even inquired about the bandanas and put in an order for one for her dog.

Indie tucked the scones into her basket, warmth blooming in her chest. She'd begun learning people's names, their families, their quirks. It wasn't just polite chatter anymore; she cared.

A gruff voice pulled her from her thoughts. "I noticed when you pulled in earlier, you've got a loose hinge on that back door."

She turned to find a fisherman staring at the baked goods. His increased face and salt-sprayed beard gave him an almost carved-from-the-sea look.

"Oh," she laughed a little, "I've been ignoring that squeak for weeks. I guess it's gotten loud enough for others to hear."

He chuckled, pointing at a Danish. "I've got the tools in the truck. I'll fix it before it falls clean off."

"Really? That's incredibly kind," Indie said, then rummaged through her basket of goods. A thought struck her, and she pulled out a delicate bracelet made of sea glass beads. "Would your wife like this? For helping me out." She had purchased it off another vendor with no real reason in mind, just that it was calling to her.

The fisherman blinked, rough hands hesitant as he accepted it. "She'll love it. It's been forty years, and I still forget gifts unless it's Christmas." His grin softened his rugged face.

"Now don't you lie, Lenard, it's definitely been fifty years." Mrs. Murphy laughed, packing his Danish.

"Forty, fifty, it's all the same after the first ten." Lenard chuckled. "I'll have your door fixed by Monday if I don't get it done before the market ends," he said to Indie, strolling off.

"Don't let Lenard fool you, he's very good to his wife, comes and buys her a Danish every Saturday. She doesn't get out much anymore, busted her hip a couple years ago on the boat and he's never forgiven himself." Indie had mixed feelings, sadness for the guilt Lenard must have felt, but also warmth from the love he had for his wife.

"That's very sweet, they must have a good story," Indie said, looking down the row of tents, watching Lenard's figure disappear.

"We all have stories to tell and stories to live, it's just about finding the place our stories belong." Mrs. Murphy smiled, turning her gaze to the couple walking up.

The moment settled deep in her bones. She felt a comfortable weight settle over her with Mrs. Murphy's words, like she was anchoring instead of drifting.

She pulled up her group chat with Lucas and Sloane.

Lucas

The Lights are still off, no answer

Poor Charlotte, what can we do?

Sloane

Form a rescue team.

Lucas

That's not funny.

Sloane

I wasn't trying to be, I mean, let's plan something.

Do you think she's ready for that?

Sloane

She's probably feeling lonely…

Like a low-key girls' night?

Lucas

I don't think she's ever done a girls' night; she probably won't show.

Frown face.

Sloane

Well, let's not give her the option. I bet your mom would help.

Lucas

> I am open to anything. Olivia misses her mom.

Later that evening, Indie padded up the steps of Charlotte's house with a mischievous determination. Josephine had promised to have Charlotte moving around by dinner. Sloane was sitting on the porch step, her bag with Butterscotch embroidered on it next to her, overflowing. The two women smiled at each other and together knocked on the door.

Charlotte answered the door, her hair tied back, dark circles smudging under her eyes.

"Sloane... Indie." She sighed. "It's late, and Josephine just took Olivia..."

"Perfect," Indie interrupted, holding up a bag of face masks, nail polish, and a box of Pop-Tarts like offerings to the gods." We're having a girls' night. Low-stakes. No leaving the house. You, Sloane, me, and Gilmore Girls reruns."

Charlotte arched an eyebrow. "This is ridiculous."

Sloane stepped into the house like she owned it. "Girl, you know you have been in here watching Gilmore Girls by yourself anyhow. Now let's party! I mean, let's relax!" Sloane pulled a bottle of wine from her bag. "One for each of us."

Charlotte hesitated, her walls creeping up... but then, maybe because she was too tired to fight or maybe because Sloane's energy was impossible to refuse, she let out a reluctant laugh. "Fine. But no waxing. I draw the line there." Indie whooped with delight and followed Charlotte in.

The house felt colder than it had the last time Indie was in it. Picture frames were empty, and the wall looked as if it had been scrubbed. Every door was closed like it was reflecting Charlotte's desire to be closed off. Somehow, the air smelled empty. She desperately wanted to light a candle to chase away the grief. Was this what her aurora felt like after she lost her mom? How long had it taken her to recover? Has she ever fully recovered? The thought ran through her mind as she followed Charlotte and Sloane down the hall to the kitchen.

"Okay, let's get cozy, I'm dying to bust open this wine." Sloane's voice chased away her thoughts. Tonight was for Charlotte to process, not for her too, right?

They sprawled across the couch with blankets, glasses of wine, and a plate of snacks. The glow of Stars Hollow filled the room as Lorelei cracked another quick-witted line.

Midway through their second episode, Indie slathered green goop across her face and turned to Charlotte. "If we're doing this, you're not staying pristine."

Charlotte snorted as Indie lunged at her with the brush. "You're insane!" She shrieked; her laughter sounded like it was just coming out of hibernation. Sloane joined in randomly tossing cucumbers on their faces.

By the time they were done, all the women had streaky masks, bright toenails, and tears in their eyes from laughing too hard.

When the laughter finally ebbed, silence settled in. The kind of silence that invited truth.

Indie toyed with the edge of her blanket. "You know... When I first started traveling, I thought freedom would feel like never needing anyone. But sometimes it just felt... lonely. Like I was shouting into the world and no one was shouting back."

Sloane nodded. "It's like we are surrounded by people, but no one hears us down in the well screaming for not even help anymore, but any morsel of real company."

Charlotte's gaze softened. "Yeah," she whispered. "That's exactly it. I called him. I have called him every day since he left. He won't answer, I'm shouting out to him, but I know he won't answer." She looked at them like she was going to say more, but stopped.

Indie nodded slowly. "When my mom died, I called her phone every day until I ran out of money for the pay phone. I knew she wouldn't answer, but there was some sort of hope that she or someone would hear the phone ringing and that if they would just answer it, everything would be fixed."

The words cracked something between them, a door swinging open.

"The house is so empty, I hate it, I hate this house. I hate looking around, knowing he designed this house to be perfect for him, and he still hated it so much he left. I have never done anything by myself; I have always had someone, and now he is gone, and I'm Olivia's only parent. I'm not good enough for her, I can't do this by myself, I'm going to be a burden to my family. I'm already a burden." Charlotte's words became faster the more she talked, and tears slid down her face. leaving streaks through the face mask.

Indie squeezed her hand. "You're not a burden. And Olivia already has everything she needs. But I get it. It's scary, loving someone so much you're terrified of failing them." Sloane slid closer to Charlotte, linking arms with her.

Charlotte blinked, trying to fight back more tears, then let out a shaky laugh. "I don't know, I can't even have a girls' night correctly."

"Don't tell anyone, but all my girl nights end with crying and dripping face masks onto the floor. I hope this doesn't stain." They dissolved into another fit of laughter, looking down at the spots of green goop dotting their blankets.

"Oh, I'm going to miss this," Sloane said offhandedly, leaning against the couch, grabbing a rag from the warm water bucket, and whipping her face.

"What do you mean?" Charlotte asked, doing the same but with a puzzled expression, her voice still cracking from her tears. Indie was also confused and stared at Sloane.

"Oh, I just mean." Sloane paused like she was trying to recover and change her thoughts that started to form. "I mean, I have missed this. It's been a while since I've been to the farm, and you know, had this kind of fun." Sloane closed her eyes. Indie's breath shortened as she looked at Charlotte, whose face started to twist in disappointment, like she caught Sloane's original thought.

"You and Lucas are still leaving," she croaked. Sloane opened her eyes, throwing an apologetic glance at Indie.

"I mean, the last time we talked." Indie scratched her arm with discomfort. She felt like she could see the walls slamming around Charlotte again. No one moved or spoke. The Gilmore Girls' intro started to play.

Charlotte's face started to turn red, as if she was holding in her anger and tears. "You need to go." Charlotte stood up.

"Char," Indie started, also standing while Sloane threw looks between the two women.

"It's Charlotte." Charlotte's voice rose. "And I mean it, get out of my house."

"Now come on..." Sloane started standing up and putting herself between Indie and Charlotte.

"No, you can go too, Sloane. Get out." Charlotte turned and seemed to run to the nearest room, slamming the door.

"I'm sorry," Sloane whispered, "I didn't think..."

"It's okay," Indie responded, but her heart dropped to her toes. "Let's clean up. Maybe she just needs more processing time." Indie gnawed on the inside of her cheek.

She pulled out her phone to text Lucas.

Just cleaning up at Charlotte's then headed out.

How did it go?

I thought it was going good, but sort of ended bad.

?

I'll see you soon.

Chapter Fifty-One

Lucas

The back patio smelled like woodsmoke and basil. Lucas worked the dough with his hands, dusting flour across the wide butcher block counter while Olivia stood on a stool beside him. Her small palms pressed down on the soft round of dough, leaving uneven imprints.

"Like this, sweetheart," Josephine said, guiding Olivia's hands with her own, gently and patiently. "Flat, like you're patting a puppy."

Olivia giggled and smashed her fist into the center. "Puppy squish!"

Lucas shook his head, smiling despite himself. "Close enough." He reached for the sauce, tomatoes he'd canned himself last summer, and spread it over his creation. Olivia dumped a mountain of mozzarella in the middle, more avalanche than sprinkle, and Lucas didn't bother fixing it.

Josephine glanced at him with that knowing softness only a mother could have. "She's making it her own. That's the best part."

Out back, the brick pizza oven glowed hot, fire licking at the sides. Lucas slid the pizzas inside with practiced ease, the smell of charcoal and bubbling cheese soon filling the air. His dad, Hank, was fussing with the projector, muttering about cables, while Josephine set a big pitcher of homemade lemonade on the picnic table.

By the time the pizzas came out crispy, steaming, imperfectly shaped but perfect all the same, the sun had melted into an opalite hue across the horizon. Fireflies blinked lazily in the yard. Lucas carried the tray out, Olivia trailing behind him with a stack of paper plates bigger than her head.

"Outdoor movie night, complete," Hank announced, finally getting the picture to flicker to life on the side of the barn. "Let's just hope the mosquitoes don't eat us alive."

They settled in on lawn chairs and quilts, plates balanced on laps. Olivia kicked off her sandals and curled against Lucas's side, already more interested in the stars appearing overhead than the movie warming up.

For a while, it was easy. Warm pizza, cool lemonade, the hum of cicadas. Family.

But then Josephine leaned closer, her voice low enough that Olivia wouldn't catch the weight of it. "You've been carrying something in your chest. I can see it."

Lucas shrugged, taking a long drink of lemonade. "It's nothing."

Josephine gave him that look. "Lucas."

He sighed, running a hand over the back of his neck. "Life has just been different, Indie... she makes things feel easy. Free."

Josephine's eyes softened, pride and worry tangled together. "Free is good for you. You've always been the one holding everything in place, since you were barely older than Olivia."

Hank leaned back in his chair, arms crossed, as his eyes stayed on the screen. "And what happens if he goes chasing after this girl and everything here falls apart? The farm, the market doesn't run itself."

Lucas frowned, but Josephine's hand found his arm, grounding him. "It's not all on him, Hank. It never should've been." She looked at her son. "Your sister's stronger than you think. She'll find her way."

Hank shook his head. "She's got her own struggles. She's not built like him. If he leaves—"

"She'll be okay," Josephine cut in gently, but firmly. "And so will we. Lucas deserves more than duty. Following your heart isn't selfish, son, it's the bravest thing you can do." Josephine gave Hank a disapproving look.

Hank grunted. Lucas knew his dad meant well; he preferred everyone to stay on the farm. He knew the farm had its legacy, but he wasn't sure if he'd be the one to carry it.

Lucas's throat felt tight. Fireflies pulsed at the edge of the yard, rising and fading like sparks. Olivia's small hand rested sticky with lemonade against his, her head heavy on his chest.

For a moment, he let himself picture what it might feel like to stop being the one holding everything together and just be free.

Chapter Fifty-Two

Indie

Indie walked out of the farmhouse with Sloane at her side, the night air cooler than it had been when they arrived. Crickets sang from the fields, and the laughter from earlier already felt like a memory she wasn't sure she'd get back.

Sloane squeezed her arm. "You okay?"

Indie forced a smile. "Yeah. She just... needs time."

She gave Sloane a hug and promised to text her later.

Her chest ached as she padded across the gravel, her bag of face masks and nail polish heavier than it had any right to be. She glanced back once, at the dark farmhouse windows, then turned her steps toward the glow she could see flickering faintly from across the yard.

Lucas's house sat in a pool of warm lamplight. Outside, a movie's closing credits rolled across the side of the barn, fireflies drifting lazily in the tall grass. Josephine was gathering plates, and Hank was folding up a quilt. Lucas was at the edge of it all, cradling Olivia, already asleep. He looked up when Indie approached, his face softening.

"Hey," he said quietly, careful not to wake Olivia.

"Hey," she echoed, her voice a little raw.

Josephine gave Indie a knowing smile as she passed by with the dishes. "We'll head to the main house. Goodnight, sweetheart." Josephine set the plates down on the porch table and reached out for Olivia. Lucas gently handed her over to his mom. Hank joined them, giving a quiet nod to Indie.

"Goodnight," Indie whispered. Indie and Lucas stood side by side, watching his parents climb into the truck and head down the gravel road.

Within moments, the yard quieted. It was just her and Lucas, the projector's glow fading into the dark, the cicadas loud in the trees. Indie sank down onto the porch step, her bag sliding to the ground.

Lucas set the cups aside and sat beside her, their shoulders brushing. "You okay?"

Indie let out a shaky laugh. "Depends on your definition. Also, I'm not sure what they are about to walk into with Charlotte, if they are going to go check on her."

For a beat, neither spoke. Finally, Lucas murmured, "Tonight... with my family... I realized I've spent so long being the one holding everything together, I forgot what it feels like to just... be free." He glanced sideways at her, his eyes steady. "With you, I get that back."

Indie's throat tightened, her chest still heavy from Charlotte's rejection, but something in his words soothed the sting. She leaned her head against his shoulder, eyes closing. "Good. Because I don't think either of us deserves to feel trapped." Indie wasn't ready to share what had happened with Charlotte yet. She walked into Lucas's arms, letting him embrace her. They both avoided each other's eyes and looked up at the stars.

The fireflies pulsed in the grass. The last of the movie credits flickered out. And for a moment, under the weight of all they couldn't yet solve, there was still this: two people, side by side, choosing the quiet freedom of each other.

NICOLE LINETTE

Chapter Fifty-Three

Lucas phone buzzed on the table, he tightened his hold on Indie as a message from Charlotte flashed on the screen.

> I can't believe you are leaving me.

NICOLE LINETTE

Chapter Fifty-Four

Indie never expected to know so many names. When she first rolled into Deer Isle, she figured she'd keep her head down, sell her soaps and everlasting flowers, and slip away before anyone noticed, like she always has. But now, on a crisp morning, walking through, she found herself calling out to residents.

"How's your mom feeling today, Mr. Robert?" She called, waving at little Maddie, who had painted a crooked rainbow across her cheeks.

The interactions, the connections brought her joy, it was as if roots were forming and they were holding her grounded to Deer Isle. The thought sent a wave of anxiety over her, she felt the familiar pressure of confinement. Her thoughts briefly spiraled. What if she messed up? What if her true self, the self that had been hurt, that cried on the inside made its way out and these people turned their nose up at her pain. She inhaled deeply, she knew that she was spiraling, she exhaled slowly.

When she looked up, she saw Mr. Roberts watching his big eyes, kind and soft as if he knew the internal struggle she was battling.

"She's great, she just wanted to give us a heart attack, apparently." He chuckled. "I hope you are well too? Not working too hard? No one is giving you any grief?"

"Oh no never, everything is great, I am starting to feel settled," Indie responded and it was mostly true the only person giving her grief was herself.

Mr. Robert smiled and nodded. "Well good, we best be going, you let me know if you need anything." He continued on pulling the girl along, who gave Indie a wide toothy grin and a small wave bye.

"Indie!" A female voice called from the other side of the road. She was pretty sure the woman's name was Caroline. "It's me, Caroline, we met at goat yoga," the woman said, looking both ways before running across the street. "I just wanted to check in, my little boy King will be starting kindergarten with Olivia. I heard about Daniel. Is he really gone?" Indie felt a little uncomfortable about discussing the Carringtons, but it seemed like the news had echoed through the town.

"Umm, I think it's a family situation." She felt a blush cross her face.

"Oh, no worries. In this small town, nothing stays family for long, especially if Hank makes a statement." She laughed, adjusting her bags. Indie gave her a puzzled look. "Oh, you know Hank, Lucas's dad, he is a strong man, you know, he did some jail time when he was young." Indie could feel her face turn down in concern. "Oh no, no nothing like terrible. No one here thinks he should have done any time. We all would have clocked the fucker if he didn't beat us to it."

"I still don't understand?" Indie said, glancing around to see who was listening.

"When Hank was younger, this big shot from Portland came strolling in. A terrible man caused lots of chaos. Hank clocked him good and ran him out. He got a couple of months." Caroline tsked. "Anyway, I heard people saw a glimpse of protector Hank when he came to collect Lucas from the bar the other night." Caroline seemed to flush thinking about it. Indie nodded slowly like she was following the conversation. "Well, I didn't mean to get caught up in everything, just wanted to make sure you were all okay, and let you know I can totally help with Olivia's school drop off and pick up, maybe we can do some play dates."

"I'll let Charlotte know. I bet Olivia would love that," Indie responded.

"Oh, perfect, I'm gonna run, but I look forward to the next goat yoga. Let's do lunch sometime, I'd love to get to know the newest Carrington member." Caroline gave a little wave and scampered away, her heels clicking on the sidewalk as she went.

Indie blinked a couple of times in confusion about the conversation. She had questions, but she also felt like the conversation was weaving her into the Carringtons' family. It was like the town knew she wasn't passing through anymore. She was part of the fabric. And to her surprise, it felt amazing.

That evening, she ended up on the Carringtons' land again, walking beside Lucas with the last of the day's sun dripping gold through the trees. Olivia had begged her to help decorate the goats with ribbons for the "Goat parade," which mostly meant they ran around laughing while Lucas shook his head, smiling.

Indie had just given up chasing Olivia and the goats around and was making her way to lean up against the barn to watch with Lucas when the sound of the four-wheel approaching caught their attention. Indie squinted, making out Josephine on the four-wheeler. She lifted her hand in a wave.

"Hey, kids," Josephine called, climbing off and heading to them.

"Gamma, look," Olivia cheered, "we did a goat parade." Olivia went over to the gate. Josephine laughed.

"Sorry, I missed all the action. I figured Olivia was getting hungry for dinner. I think Charlotte wants to take her out for hamburgers." Josephine's eyes were full of love as she looked at her granddaughter. Olivia's face matched the relief Indie felt that Charlotte was starting to interact with people again. Charlotte hadn't texted her, and as far as she knew, Charlotte hadn't texted Lucas either, well, not since girls' night. Indie still felt guilty for how it ended, but maybe Charlotte taking Olivia out for burgers meant it helped. Indie felt Lucas's gaze on her, and she looked up at him, giving him a small smile.

"Well, that's a great plan," Lucas replied, looking back at Josephine and Olivia. "Off you go, bug," he was saying as she was scaling the fence and jumping into Josephine's arms.

"Cheeseburger, cheeseburger," Olivia chanted as they moved to the four-wheeler, Josephine laughing and giving them a wave goodbye.

Lucas motioned to the truck. "Let's head to my place." Indie nodded.

The crickets sang. A low fire crackled in the pit, and he handed her a mug of warm cider. They didn't need to fill the silence; it felt safe, like the kind that wrapped you up instead of pushed you out. Indie breathed in the smells around her, letting her eyes drift closed as she thought about breaking the silence.

"You look cozy," Lucas commented. She opened an eye to find him staring.

"Cozier if you had a couch out here vs chairs, or if you had a hammock. There's surprisingly a lack of hammocks around the farm," she joked. Lucas laughed.

"I'll work on that," he patted his lap, "you can come sit in this chair with me in the meantime." Indie felt herself blush but moved to sit with him. She lay her head against his shoulder, and he pulled the blanket up around her.

"I ran into Caroline," Indie said, feeling like she was melting into him.

"Oh yeah?" Lucas's voice was soft and relaxed.

"She called me the newest member of the Carringtons." She lightly laughed, not wanting to break the coziness.

"You're getting yourself tangled up with this place," Lucas said finally, his voice low, almost cautious. She could feel his heart beating against her.

Indie smiled into his chest. "Maybe I like being tangled." She wanted to ask about the bar, but she also wanted to hold on to this moment. She inhaled her scent and decided that if it were important, Lucas would have mentioned it.

Chapter Fifty-Five

Lucas

Lucas's chest tightened. Guilt had been twisting in his stomach since he left Charlotte's message unread. He wanted to tell Indie they should stay instead of traveling. To admit how much lighter the farm felt with her laugh bouncing off the barn walls, how even his bees seemed calmer when she was near. But he couldn't ask her for something she might not want to give. He was battling between losing his sister and losing the woman whom he was starting to think was the love of his life.

He held Indie a little tighter, letting the warmth of her body consume him. If he could turn off his brain and just be in this moment with her, it would be perfect. The fire was crackling, the crickets singing, the stars shining. Indie, breathing calmly in his arms, he could never ask for a more perfect moment, if only he could let the guilt go.

The moon was high when Lucas finally let out a long exhale, he could smell the storm rolling in. "We should head in," he whispered shifting slightly adjusting her weight in his arms.

"Boo," Indie responded in a whisper like he had disrupted her sleep. He looked down at her, her eyes looked sleepy and the moonlight highlighted her face. He leaned over planting a kiss on her forehead.

"You can spend the night, if you want to." He brushed some hair from her forehead. "I have to get up early tomorrow, there's a storm coming in." Indie stretched in his lap before moving to stand. He wanted to grab her and pull her back down to him.

"I'd love to. but I left some flowers hanging outside before I came over. I should go store them, it's going to rain." She held out her hand to him.

He grasped her hand and rose to his feet pulling her into him. He wrapped her in a hug. "Let's just stay here for a minute and take in the night." He caught himself, the guilt returning stabbing him in the heart.

She nodded quietly, resting her head on his chest. He swayed them like there was a slow song playing. He could hear Indie humming lightly, the sound vibrating against his chest. Maybe if he never let go he would never have to return to reality that he had to decide between abandoning his sister or potentially losing his heart.

NICOLE LINETTE

Chapter Fifty-Six

Indie

That night, it took all of Indie's strength to pry herself from Lucas and return to her trailer; her heart was brimming. She wasn't sure what came over her Lucas wrapping her in his arms, but she started to hum *I'll be Home for Christmas*, as they swayed under the moonlight. She was surprised she still remembered the song.

She thought of the last time her mother and her hummed to the song playing on the old record player. Her mom was unfolding the fake Christmas tree from the box, their home smelt like pine and cinnamon from the candles they had burning. Indie remembers staring at herself in the hand mirror.

"Stop poking your face, my love, you're turning yourself red." Her mother's voice came clearly to her.

She tossed the mirror down, eyes brimming with tears. She remembered her mother cradling her in her arms whispering comforting words as Indie bawled over her appearance. She couldn't remember what her mother had said, but it was a pivotal moment, the moment she decided it was okay to be different from her peers and someday someone would love her for her.

She laughed lightly as she gathered her supplies and piled them into the van. She felt like the song came to her the moment she decided that she had found the person, and the town that accepted her. As she climbed into bed and drifted to sleep for the first time in years, she didn't dream of the next road, the next town; she was dreaming of staying and building a life.

Roots & Roadmaps

NICOLE LINETTE

Chapter Fifty-Seven

By dawn, Lucas had already decided: he couldn't leave. He spent all night lying awake, staring at the ceiling in indecision, keeping sleep away.

He said it to himself the way you say a prayer you're not sure you believe in. I can't leave. Not now. Not with Charlotte still moving through the house like a ghost, not with Olivia clinging to him in the evenings, asking if he'd still be there in the morning. The hives that his family needed him for, the east fence was bowing, and a storm was coming in. The work was endless. It always has been. But now it felt like the only language he knew how to speak.

He typed and deleted three different texts to Indie.

Can we talk?

I don't think I can—

I'm sorry.

What finally went through was the smallest, safest thing.

Busy today. Storm prep.

Her reply came quickly and warmly anyway.

Need a hand?

His chest pinched. He stared at the screen until the typing dots vanished, then set the phone face down on a hay bale and went to work until the muscles in his back burned and the ache chased out his thoughts.

The storm clouds were rolling in, casting shadows over the field. The farmhands watched him with curiosity. It had been a while since he joined them in the field; typically, he kept to his own projects. By lunch, no drops had fallen, but the sky was ominous, a reflection of his own internal battles. Lucas made his way back to his goats before he decided to sit for a break. He had a number of messages from Indie.

Hope you're okay.

Looks like it's going to be a big one.

Ran into Leonard, his wife loves the sea-glass charms.

Do you know Brandon, that teenager?

The one with the skateboard, he broke his wrist in two spots!

Deer Isle could really use a skate park.

Hope you are okay.

Pride swelled, and fear rose with it. She fit here too well. She fit everywhere. He couldn't bring himself to respond to her.

He wanted to say, stay. He wanted to say, I'm scared I'll ask, and you'll be kind enough to say yes and resent me for it later. So instead, he said nothing.

By dusk, his body was screaming; he had not pushed himself this hard in a while, but he had to stay busy. Any time his mind started to drift to Indie, the conversation with his mother screamed at him. Was he doing exactly what she warned him against? Part of him believed he was doing what was best for Indie, but the other part screamed he was trying to abandon her just like everyone else. The thoughts were tearing him apart, so instead of listening to them, he drove further into his work.

Chapter Fifty-Eight

She had woken up that morning ready to give him everything.

The words had been lined up like bright lights in her head: Let's stay. Let's revisit traveling later. Your family needs you. I want this, too. I want you. She'd walked into the day buoyant.

And then he'd gone quiet. She had sent him a number of texts with no responses. She could see the cloud rolling in, and maybe it was more serious for farmers than she thought. She replayed the night's events, sitting by the fire, and couldn't recall any significant events that would have led to radio silence. Concern was flaring in her bones as she paced around the campsite. She thought of her conversation with Olivia over their afternoon tea and strolls: Are you gonna stay forever? Indie had ruffled the girl's hair, dodged the word forever, and said I'll be here as long as you need me. She'd meant it, but maybe Olivia did not actually need her; she did have a whole family. Maybe she was just the weed in the garden that was the Carringtons.

She felt as if she should leave; the urge to run was the strongest it had been in months. She had a sinking feeling that Lucas was emotionally distancing himself. If she was trying to break away from someone or had something to say and wasn't sure how to say it, she'd ignore texts, too.

Instead of packing her belongings and hitting the road, she drove to Sloane's with rain freckling the windshield and her thoughts loud as thunder.

She strolled into Sloane's apartment as if she owned the place, sinking onto the couch and wrapping herself in her favorite fluffy blanket. Sloane peeked around the corner, unfazed.

"Indie? Give me one second, I have tea on."

When Sloane joined her on the couch, skimming through Indie and Lucas's text chain, the words exploded from Indie, "He is not responding, it's just radio silence. I think it's all too much for him, with Charlotte and Olivia, maybe I'm too much. I was going to stay, I was going to tell him I wanted to stay." She could feel the tears forming in her eyes. "We danced last night, and I thought, and I thought we were good, but maybe I hurt Charlotte, and now she's convinced him I'm no good. So now he doesn't know how to respond to me." She felt the anxiety and the feeling of inadequacy swelling inside her.

"Okay, now, take a deep breath," Sloane interrupted her, placing her warm hand on Indie's. "I have a couple of thoughts before we go down this spiral of thoughts. Indie nodded, dabbing her eyes with her palm. "You want my honest opinion?" Sloane asked, leaning back in her chair next to Indie, a cup of tea steaming from the armrest.

"Yes," Indie said, her voice sounding meek to her own ears. Outside, thunder rolled like barrels.

"Okay." Sloane picked up her mug, cradling it in her hands. "He's being a chicken shit."

Indie blinked. "That's... succinct." She almost let out a nervous chuckle.

"Men like him." She paused. "Good men sometimes think martyrdom is the same as love." Sloane's eyes were kind even as her words were sharp. "He's pulling back because he's either concerned or made a decision he doesn't think you can handle. He thinks he's saving you."

Indie swallowed. "You got all that from my unanswered messages?"

"I also think maybe you're having some big reactions from your own trauma. I get it, it sucks he's not answering, but it doesn't mean you did anything wrong, or that you are no good. You are worthy of love; have some trust in that." Indie sensed that Sloane wasn't done; she dabbed at her eyes again, watching Sloane closely and nodding along. Sloane was probably right; it was probably her own trauma causing these anxious thoughts.

Sloane leaned forward, elbows on her knees. "For a functional, beautiful family, the Carringtons are so…" She hummed, changing her mind. "Sometimes they think they are doing their best to protect, but maybe don't give others credit for being able to handle hard things." She leaned back again. "Not that I don't love them, ugh, to be a part of their family would be amazing," she said as she sipped her tea.

Lightning flared, whitening the kitchen. Indie looked down at her hands, ink-stained, calloused, the hands of a woman who'd built a life that ebbed and flowed.

"So what do I do?" Indie looked at her hands; they were steady, even with butterflies in her stomach.

"You know where he lives." She shrugged, setting her cup down and going to the coat rack. Sloane grabbed a raincoat and tossed it at her. "Go get your farmer. With the storm rolling, I assume he's with his goats or on the east side of the property."

Indie barked out a laugh that was half sob. "You're insufferable."

"And always right. Text me when you've kissed in the rain."

Under Lightening Filled Skies

NICOLE LINETTE

Chapter Fifty-Nine

Indie

By the time Indie turned up at the Carringtons' drive, the sky had split wide. Rain came in sheets, the wipers slapping wildly, lightning raking the horizon. The barn door glowed like a hearth in the dark. She stopped outside the barn, watching him, but refusing to go in from the rain.

He was there... of course he was. He had his sleeves shoved to his elbows, forearms slick, jaw set like he could muscle the weather into obedience.

"Lucas," she called over the drumming roof. Her voice shook; the resolve didn't.

He didn't turn. "Can't do this right now, I told Lauren I'd meet him."

Indie took two steps closer, water spooling from her hair to her shoulders. "Lauren can wait."

"He can't, actually." Lucas grabbed for his coat, still avoiding her eyes. "You should just go." She had never heard his voice so hard.

"Stop." The word cracked sharper than the thunder. "Stop walking away from me." She was shocked as her own voice rose.

He froze then, shoulders tight, rain pattering off the brim of his hat. Slowly, he faced her. The storm outside had nothing on the one in his eyes.

"I get storm prep, but there has to be more going on," Indie said, voice high with rain and heat. "You can't just tell me to go away," the words poured from her. "You don't get to ghost me! I deserve more respect than that."

He flinched, like the words had weight. She pressed on, breathless. "I thought I meant more to you than just someone passing through. I thought we were going to travel through this part of our lives together."

"That's the problem." Lucas's voice shook. He tossed his coat on the ground. Indie flinched slightly; she could feel her eyes welling with tears. He took a step forward but hesitated. "Indie, I can't leave. I thought I could, but my family needs me. I can't leave them. I can't pack up and go with you, I can't live the way you do, and I might not ever be able to." He looked exhausted.

"You think the road is the love of my life, and it was for a long time. But it doesn't laugh at my stupid jokes or run toward me across a field with a crooked flower crown. It didn't sit on a farmhouse porch and make everything quiet in the right ways.

You did. This family did." A tear mingled with rain and down her cheek leading the taste of salt on her lips.

"I was going to tell you this morning," she said, softer now. "That I want to stay. That we can revisit traveling another time. I can't imagine being anywhere else right now, because I'm tired of chasing lines on a map. I want roots. Here. With you." She took a shaky breath. "So stop deciding I'll leave just because that's who I was yesterday."

For a heartbeat, nothing moved. Even the rain seemed to catch.

Then Lucas's face crumpled. He curled a hand into his hair; his voice sounded like he was fighting back a sob. "God, Indie." He stepped toward her, closing the distance, and she watched the rain soak his hair. "I'm sorry. I thought I was sparing you. I thought if I told you I had to stay, you'd... choose the road without me, and it would hurt too much." His voice broke. "I didn't trust that you'd choose me."

She stood frozen, the words hurt, she felt like she could trust him, but somehow, he couldn't trust her. "I didn't mean for you not to trust me."

He reached for her then, and she threw herself into his arms. "I trust you, it's not that I don't trust you," he whispered, holding her tighter, and the tears rolled from her eyes. "It's not you, I was just afraid. You are so important to me." Her tears fell faster, mixing with the rain that was soaking them. He lightened his grip and tilted her head up, locking their lips.

The kiss was all apology and relief and the kind of certainty that remakes you. He cupped her face and kissed her again, deeper, and she tasted rain and honey and every word they hadn't said until now.

"I'm sorry," he murmured against her mouth. "For the silence. For making you carry this alone."

"Just don't do it again. You are important to me, too."

"I will never do it again." He lifted her and walked to the barn. Indie slid one hand, threw his hair, and kept the other around his neck as he continued to kiss deeply.

Thunder cracked, and lightning lit the barn as Lucas pushed her back against the barn wall. She shifted to put her legs around his waist. Her body shook with pleasure, as if she was immune to the cold, wet clothes. Lucas let out a moan as she stroked her tongue on the roof of his mouth.

"In the barn, we should." Her words were jumbled, but he seemed to catch her meaning. He let her legs fall to the ground and created enough space to unbutton her shirt. He slid her shirt off before attending to her bra. His face blushed as he looked at her breasts rather than her face. His hands hovered over her pants button. She nodded, and he went to work. It was not an easy task for two adults soaked in rain and riding the ecstasy of reconnection to undress each other, but they managed. Lucas frantically pulled her hair back, teasing her nipples with his tongue, and she had returned the favor. As he plunged into her, it felt as if he was making up for every lost second missed with her. She moaned in pleasure as release rippled through her body. Lucas responded, moaning her name, and it had never sounded so perfect.

NICOLE LINETTE

Chapter Sixty

Lucas

They ran from his truck to the house, laughter torn away by the wind, boots slapping through puddles. Inside the mudroom, they wrestled with rain ponchos they found in the bar, as neither of them could get their wet clothes back on. Indy's body did nothing to hide the fact that they had just had sex in the barn, and all it did was make him want her more. They moved with urgency like the sex in the barn was healing, but this was rejoicing. Hands steadied, and they worshiped each other as they stumbled to his room. The thunder was becoming a far-off drum, and the rain a hush. They moved together as if becoming one, they laughed and teased, until Lucas could no longer hold himself back.

Afterwards, he slipped out of bed and returned with snacks and hot tea. "Bath's running," he said, voice low, thumb brushing her cheek. "And tea, sweetened with good honey."

She smiled, eyes glassy. "You're dangerous," she whispered. "I never thought I'd feel comfortable staying in one spot. Letting my guard down and trusting someone to not throw me away, but that's how I feel with you."

He brushed a damp curl behind her ear. "I will be here with you every step of the way. I'll be here for your dark days, your mediocre days, and your happy days. I love you no matter the mood."

He helped her into the bath, the room fogging warm around them. When she lifted the mug, the citrus and honey rose up like comfort. Lucas perched on the tub's edge, towel around his waist, fingers combing gently through her hair.

She looked up at him, steady. "I'm choosing you, Lucas. I'm choosing here."

His throat worked. "Then I'm choosing to believe you. Roadmaps can wait," he whispered as he leaned in and kissed her forehead.

She took his hand and squeezed. "Roots," she said, smiling. Into the steam. "Let's grow them."

Outside, the storm was dwindling. Inside, it felt quieter, warmer, built on words neither of them would swallow again.

A Place to Belong

NICOLE LINETTE

Chapter Sixty-One

The morning after the storm was bright and impossibly clear, as if the sky itself had scrubbed away the night's heaviness. The farmhouse windows glowed with sunlight, and the air smelled sharp with wet grass and earth.

Indie stirred beneath the quilt, the familiar weight of Lucas's arm draped over her waist. His steady breathing rumbled against her back; she felt completely anchored. Not restless. Not half-packed in her mind. Just... here. She let herself drift back to sleep.

When she finally slipped from bed, she found him already in the kitchen, barefoot and quiet, pouring steaming coffee into two mismatched mugs. The sight made her chest ache. He glanced up, his eyes soft but shy in the early light.

"Morning," he said, handing her a mug and placing a kiss on her forehead.

"Good morning." She wrapped her fingers around it, the heat sinking into her palms. "You make a decent storm shelter, you know," Indie said with a wink, referring to his body.

The corner of his mouth tugged upward, just enough to show he'd heard the tease. "Glad to be of service."

They sipped in silence for a moment, the kind that felt comfortable. Then Lucas set his mug down, as if he'd made a decision.

"Come with me. I want to show you something."

They walked by the trees Indie once hid behind and into the far edge of the property, where wild grasses grew tall, and the sound of Olivia's distant laughter drifted on the breeze. Lucas's stride was sure, his hand brushing hers every so often, until he led her down a narrow path shaded by birch and pine.

They came out into a clearing she hadn't noticed before, a sloping patch of land tucked between an old apple orchard and a cluster of maples. The trees stretched wide, their branches tangled, the ground dotted with stubborn wildflowers that had fought their way up through years of neglect.

Indie turned in a slow circle, taking it in. Sunlight pooled around her, golden and soft. It felt... private. Special.

Lucas shifted beside her, suddenly uncertain. "This part of the farm hasn't been used in years. Too far from the main fields, I guess. But I always thought it could be something more."

She glanced at him, sensing the weight in his voice.

He scratched the back of his neck. "If you're really staying... maybe it could be yours. A place to make your own." She watched him shift his weight from foot to foot.

The words hit harder than she expected. Her throat tightened, eyes stinging. It wasn't just about land; it was about him, offering her a space that could be hers, like he was telling her he was fully committed to her.

Her gaze swept over the slope again, but this time her mind began to fill in the empty spaces. She could almost see a small farm stand tucked under the maples, a cheerful wooden booth painted in soft colors, with baskets of flowers spilling over the edges. Jars of honey glinting like amber in the sun. Handmade signs, little chalkboard menus, Olivia helping with change, and greeting neighbors.

A place people might linger, sip lemonade, share gossip, and feel at home.

Her chest swelled, vision blurring with possibility. "Lucas..." Her voice wavered. She swallowed, pressing her palm to his chest. "This means more than I can even say. Will your parents mind?"

He caught her hand, folding it in his, and gave it a gentle kiss. "Not at all. I brought it up with them and they loved the idea."

She leaned up and kissed him, slow and lingering, the kind of kiss that tasted of sunlight and possibility. Around them, the farm whispered in the breeze, as though blessing the moment.

On the walk back, Lucas's house came into view again, shining from the rain, fields humming with late summer life. Olivia's small figure tore across the grass the moment she spotted them, curls bouncing, grin wide. Josephine and Hank stood next to their SUV waiting for them.

"What are you smiling about?" she demanded as she barreled into Lucas.

He scooped her up with a grunt, and Indie laughed, walking beside them as they headed toward the house. Lucas had Olivia clinging to his shoulders, Indie at his side, and for one fleeting heartbeat, she felt as if she already belonged to this family.

And deep in her chest, a quiet certainty bloomed: This wasn't just a place to pass through, it was a place to build from.

Chapter Sixty-Two

Lucas

Lucas smiled at his parents. He felt relieved that Indie wanted to stay. He led Indie to his parents while carrying Olivia.

"Everything alright?" he asked, setting Olivia down in the driveway.

"Yeah, we were driving by and wanted to let you know we are taking Olivia out today. Charlotte is back at her house if you want to swing by," Hank responded as if commanding him to talk to her.

"We thought maybe you and Indie could both go over there, maybe take her some brunch?" Josephine smiled, making tickling fingers at Olivia, who was running in circles. Lucas nodded slowly.

"I think that's a lovely idea," Indie filled in the space. "We can maybe pick up some scones and mimosas." Indie clapped her hands together. He loved the way she could take charge.

Forty-five minutes later, Lucas pulled into Charlotte's driveway. He hadn't been back to the house since the girls had their girls' night. Indie touched his arm.

"Are you ready?" she asked softly. He nodded.

"I don't know why I'm nervous. I've known Charlotte my whole life."

"You don't know heartbroken Charlotte, though. She's in a transitional space; it's hard, but you can be there for her even if you aren't actively doing anything," she said.

"Okay, let's do this," he said as he got out of the truck, grabbing the grocery bags, while Indie got out, taking the scones. He gently knocked on the door before entering. "Hey, Charlotte, it's Lucas and Indie."

"I know the sound of your truck, Lucas. You don't have to announce yourself," Charlotte barked from the dining room. Lucas glanced at Indie, and she smiled encouragingly, lacing their fingers together, and he led the way to the dining room.

Papers and pictures were scattered over the table. Charlotte looked tired but had more color in her face than the last time he saw her. He set the bags on the island. Indie went to work, pulling out the items and opening the box of scones.

"We brought mimosas and scones," Indie said softly with a smile, then added, "and news."

Charlotte's head shot up, and she stared at Lucas. "Yeah, we talked, and we are gonna stay." Charlotte's brows knit together. "Like both me and Indie are staying in Deer Isle." Charlotte's eyes welled with tears, and she pushed back from her chair. Lucas went to her and held her as she cried.

"I don't want you to resent me for making you stay, but I don't want to lose you," she sobbed. Lucas held her tighter but looked up, making eye contact with Indie.

"I understand that feeling, but you can't shut me out because of your fear; you have to trust me to do what is right for me and for our family." Lucas smiled at Indie, who smiled back.

"We aren't ready to go anywhere," Indie added, joining in the group hug. Charlotte's body seemed to shake with relief.

After a long, quiet moment, the three of them split apart. Indie moved to mix mimosas, and Charlotte returned to her seat. Lucas took a seat across from her.

"What's going on here?" He tried to keep his face neutral.

"I... I was trying to see if I missed something." She looked down. Lucas saw her cheeks turn a different shade of pink, not from tears but embarrassment, maybe.

"Tell me more?"

"Like maybe I should have noticed Daniel was unhappy before." She shuffled through pictures nervously. Indie sat down on a plate of scones near Charlotte.

"As someone who has been around a lot of very unhappy people. I can tell you, sometimes it's easy to hide. He could have talked with you, but he was being childish; this is not on you. He was lucky to have you for as long as he did." Indie started to gather the papers, Charlotte's hand held tightly to one of her wedding photos. Lucas watched, unsure what to do.

"You had a lot of wonderful memories, don't go second-guessing every moment. Let the good memories stay good, and use this new information to influence the present, not the past." Indie placed her hands on Charlotte's shoulder.

"I just don't know how to come back from this." Her voice cracked, and she reached for her mimosa. Chugging it, while tears rolled down her face.

"You don't have to rush; it will take time, but you will recover," Indie stated, taking a seat.

"And we can help you," Lucas added, trying to show support for what Indie was saying. Charlotte nodded slowly.

"I think I want to re-paint the house." Her comment surprised Lucas.

"What?"

"I don't like the greys and cool colors, I want orange, creams, yellows." Charlotte smiled softly. "I want this to feel more like my home."

"I will tear down, rebuild, and repaint anything you want me to. We should have never let him dismiss the dreams you had for this house." Both women smiled at Lucas, and he felt at peace. This was going to be fine, Charlotte was going to heal, Indie was going to stay, and he... well, he would get to keep doing what he always did, be predictable, sturdy, and work hard.

NICOLE LINETTE

Chapter Sixty-Three

Indie paced behind Charlotte who moved with determi-nation through the store. Charlotte had handfuls of color swatches. Indie smiled, watching her lift the cream color she found, comparing it to other cheerful colors.

"How about this orange? I think it will brighten up the dining room. Maybe Lucas can replace the window. I would kill for a bigger window in the dining room."

"I think that's a great color." Indie was honestly enjoying her time with Charlotte; the woman seemed to be coming back to herself, but she knew this was just a good moment and that Charlotte had a long road of healing. Indie thought about the first time she was told her placement was disrupted; she had been confused, scared even. She didn't understand why the couple had been sending her away. She replayed the month over and over in her head and had no clues as to what she had done wrong. She found out later that the couple was waiting for placement of a baby, and they were just emergency placements for her. It was like a stipulation: we will show you affection and care for you, but only for this short while, then we will push you out the door with the dust bunnies. That was the only place she had really felt at ease. Following that move, she remembered bitterness growing in her; she felt on alert, like a kind of animal being moved from shelter to shelter, not given time to rest and find sanctuary.

Now watching Charlotte explore paint, and discuss house detail, Indie felt a little jealous that her only canvas for such things was her van and trailer. She wondered what it would be like as an adult to paint a wall however she desired.

"Indie... Indie, you there?" Charlotte's words broke her thoughts.

"Oh, sorry, I was thinking about what it would be like to paint a room." She blushed with embarrassment. Charlotte's brows raised.

"Well, I figured you would help me paint... maybe." Her words seemed unsure.

"Oh no, of course, I definitely am going to help you," she spoke in a higher tone, trying to display excitement. Charlotte seemed to notice she had another meaning. Charlotte cleared her throat.

"You know I do have that guest room, maybe you could decorate it. I'm sure you have seen way more interesting places than I, and I'd love to have a space that sort of brought traveling or exploring to my home." Charlotte looked away from Indie. "I want Olivia to grow up knowing there's more out there than Deer Isle."

Indie smiled. "I would love to help you make that space."

Charlotte seemed to laugh out of discomfort. "I'm sure Lucas would let you do anything to his house that you want." She laughed a little louder.

Indie thought about it. The statement felt true; maybe she could make Lucas's home into their home. She was planning on staying for him, so it seemed... Reasonable.

NICOLE LINETTE

Old Ghosts & New Roots

NICOLE LINETTE

Chapter Sixty-Four

The late summer air carried the hum of cicadas as Indie arranged jars of wildflower honey and lavender bundles on the market table. She hummed under her breath, trying not to notice how Lucas's hand brushed against hers as he set out a crate of sun-bright tomatoes. Everything felt steady again between them. After the rain-soaked confessions, it felt like they were moving forward. Charlotte's house had been repainted, and Hank, as they worked, was tearing Charlotte's bedroom to the bones and rebuilding, justifying that he could smell the disgust of Daniel in the walls. Indie and Lucas had spent a couple of evenings with Charlotte planning an all-season room to add off the dining room. Charlotte was hyper-focused on the house, which may have been what she needed to help process Daniel's disappearance.

"Lucas?" a low, calm female voice broke Indie's thoughts. Indie turned, and her stomach did a strange little flip.

The woman standing at the edge of their booth looked like she had stepped out of a glossy farm lifestyle magazine, sun-kissed and hair tucked under a wide-brimmed hat, fitted jeans, and a confident smile. Her eyes lit up as she saw Lucas.

"Ashley?" His voice carried both surprise and warmth.

They hugged, and Indie suddenly felt like the ground tilted beneath her.

Ashley shook it firmly. "Nice to meet you. I'm Ashley, and Lucas and I go way back. I just got back from Colorado. Finally finished my master's in agricultural science." She clapped her hands with joy. "Thought I'd stop by and see how the old place was doing."

Indie plastered on a smile. "Hi, I'm Indie." She stuck out her hand, the vendor charm in her voice steady even though her pulse skittered.

Agricultural science. Of course. Indie's mind twisted with the words useful, practical, impressive. Unlike making flower bracelets and carving soap in a lavender VW bus.

"Wow," Indie said brightly. "That's... amazing. You two should catch up. I've got a few errands, anyway." She felt uneasy; was this jealousy? This was too new, too much for her.

Lucas frowned, looking as if he was about to protest, but Indie pressed a quick kiss to his cheek. "Really. Catch up. And no more free samples to Mr. Lenard, I think he's just collecting all the samples to build a block of soap for a gift." She laughed, skipping away, nervous, shaking her body, and her heart pounding.

At Sloane's kitchen counter, Indie tore strips of fabric for a patchwork project, but Butterscotch was purring on her lap like he knew she needed to be grounded. The storm of insecurity inside her swelled.

"She's... perfect," Indie muttered, pulling too hard on the fabric. It ripped unevenly.

Sloane poured coffee and sat across from her, one eyebrow arched. "Perfect? Or just polished?" Sloane sounded like she had a hint of amusement in her voice.

Indie huffed. "She has a degree in farm things, Sloane. Farm things! I can barely tell the difference between the two kinds of squash. What if he realizes she's more... right for him?"

Sloane leaned forward. "Indie, Lucas doesn't need someone who knows how to write a soil analysis. He needs someone who sees him when he's quiet, who makes him laugh, who isn't afraid to challenge him. He doesn't need a farmhand with a diploma. He needs you. Plus, didn't you all just have your kiss in the rain confess everything moment?"

Indie bit her lip, eyes stinging. "But she knew him first."

Sloane softened. "And he chose you second. Which means he knew better the second time."

Indie let out a watery laugh, wiping her cheek. But the anxious knot inside her still tugged.

Sloane continued, "Plus, it was a mutual ending. If I remember, there was no chemistry; that spark just didn't ignite." Sloane laughed at herself.

"That was cheesy." Indie laughed, and Sloane flicked a piece of cubed cheese at her.

"This is cheesy. But honest, babe, I think you're letting your own trauma influence you on this one." Indie crinkled her nose. Sloane was probably right; she had a history of being right. She looked down at the still, patchy old man cat and gave him a scratch on the ear.

Chapter Sixty-Five

Lucas leaned against the fence rail at the farm, listening as Ashley recounted her years out west, research projects, sustainable farming initiatives, professors who pushed her to think bigger. She was animated, smart, and confident. The girl he'd once thought he'd build a future with.

But as she spoke, Lucas realized something. He didn't feel that pull anymore. She was part of his past, someone who had shaped who he was. But his future, his roots, his heart, wasn't in old memories.

It was with Indie.

"You seem distracted," Ashley noted, sipping from her beer. "Anything to do with that little redhead that ran off like I was the plague."

Lucas chuckled lightly. "Maybe, I'm just thinking about how much she means to me."

"Glad my stories bored you enough to realize you loved the girl." Ashley laughed, slapping him on the shoulder. He felt his face grow serious. Was Ashley right? "Hey, now don't go all serious, all I'm saying is you seem lighter and she seems very breezy, she's probably good for you."

"I think you're right," Lucas said, shocked. "I think I do love her." Ashley laughed again.

"You honestly were never good at figuring out obvious things if it didn't involve the farm," she said, rolling her eyes. "You should go tell her that you love her." Lucas stood up from the fence, leaving his beer on the rail.

"You're right, but this is different. I need to go tell her." He whipped his hand on his jeans, a restless urgency rising in his chest. He had let Indie walk away, probably thinking the worst.

"You do you, bud, but there's no rush. I don't think she's going anywhere." She chugged back her beer. "I'm gonna run before I convince you to propose to the woman."

Chapter Sixty-Six

Indie sat cross-legged on Sloane's porch swing, Butterscotch curled beside her, pretending to focus on stitching when Lucas's truck pulled up the drive.

He didn't hesitate, just walked straight to her, eyes soft but serious. "Indie."

Her throat tightened. "How was catching up?"

Lucas crouched in front of her, shaking his head. "It was fine. But all I kept thinking was how much I wanted to be with you instead."

Her lip trembled, and he took her hands, fabric scraps falling to the porch.

"You're my present, Indie. My future. Ashley's just... Someone I used to know. But you're the one I don't ever want to imagine not knowing."

Indie exhaled a shaky laugh, tears slipping free. "You always know exactly when to say the right thing, don't you?"

"Not always." He smiled faintly. "But with you, I want to get it right."

She leaned forward, pressing her forehead against his. The insecurities melted in the warmth of his words, in the truth she felt in his touch.

Sloane's voice broke the moment from the doorway. "If you two are going to cry on my porch, at least let me get tissues and popcorn." Butterscotch stretched from his spot at the sound of Sloane's voice and slowly wandered inside, like Indie and Lucas were insignificant to her.

Indie laughed through her tears, Lucas's arms circling around her. The old ghosts of doubt had faded. What remained was solid, rooted, and real.

Chapter Sixty-Seven

Lucas

That night, Lucas and his dad walked the fence line. He hadn't been able to bring himself to tell Indie he loved her on Sloane's porch; he felt like there was a better place and time for it.

"I'm proud of the choice you made," his dad said, his deep voice vibrating through the evening air.

"Yeah, I just think it's for the best for me to stay." He shrugged.

"Yeah, you have always been a hard worker." His dad paused, looking out over the pasture. "I think this woman, Indie, might help you loosen up a little, maybe have more fun."

Lucas's stomach turned. "I don't know, there's a lot to do, I can't have too much fun." He scuffed his boot on the ground. "I think I'll still be useful."

"Lucas, my boy, you have always been dependable, and usefulness is not all you are."

Lucas wasn't sure why he said it, but the words tumbled out of his mouth. "When I was younger, I heard you. You and Mom in the kitchen talking about having to hire hands because I was too much," he summarized, looking down.

"What?" Hank sounded shocked. "I can promise you that never happened."

"Mom said she needed help with me, and you said we couldn't afford it. I was a burden." Lucas tried to stay calm; he felt hurt that, in such an important moment in his life, his dad couldn't remember.

"No, Lucas, Look at me." Lucas raised his head. "That was not about you, my boy, and I am sorry if this has been weighing you down." He cleared his throat. "We never talked to you or Charlotte about it, but you were going to have a younger sibling, your mom swore it was a little boy even picked out the name Benjamin." He cleared his throat again, like it was hard to talk about. "Your mom lost the baby. I should have gotten the farmhands. I don't know if it would have made a difference, but she asked, and I should have." Lucas could hear the pain in his dad's voice. Clarity blossomed through him, but also grief for the childhood memories he felt like he had lost.

"I... I don't know what to say." Suddenly, Lucas felt his dad's arms around him, and he hugged him back.

"Promise me you will try to lighten up. I know I was skeptical of Indie, but I have never seen you so at rest with yourself." His dad stepped back, holding him at arm's length. "I want you to be more than this farm." Lucas nodded.

NICOLE LINETTE

Blueberry-stained Promises

NICOLE LINETTE

Chapter Sixty-Eight

Indie leaned over the counter, squinting at the mixing bowl as if it might reveal its secrets if she stared hard enough. "So, what exactly makes this pie so famous? Is it the blueberries? The crust? Or are you guarding the recipe like a dragon with its treasure?"

Lucas chuckled, rolling up his sleeves. "It's the crust. My grandmother swore it had to be made with just the right ratio of butter to flour, and you have to work it fast so it doesn't get tough."

"So basically magic," Indie said, nodding solemnly. She dipped her hands into the flour, immediately sending up a cloud that settled into her hair. She coughed, waving a hand in front of her face. "Okay, maybe not magic, maybe witchcraft."

"Definitely witchcraft," Lucas said, reaching past her to grab the butter. His arm brushed hers, warm and steady, and Indie tried not to notice how her heart skipped.

She dug both hands into the flour and butter mixture, working it the way Lucas had shown her. Within moments, though, it was less working the dough and more accidents flinging it across the counter. "Oh no," she groaned, watching a small clump roll to the floor.

Lucas snorted. "That's not exactly how Grandma did it."

Indie gave him a mock glare, then, before she could stop herself, flicked a pinch of flour at him. It landed on his dark T-shirt, like fresh fallen snow.

His eyebrows shot up. "Did you just?"

"Yes," she said, biting back a grin. "And I'd do it again."

In a flash, his hand scooped into the flour tin and dusted her cheek with a bold swipe. Indie squealed, staggering back with her hands in the air. "Unfair! You have farmer reflexes!"

"You started it." His grin widened as he advanced.

Within seconds, it was chaos. Indie tried to dodge around him, but Lucas caught her wrist, gently pulling her back. Their laughter filled the kitchen as she wriggled free just enough to smear her flour covered palm down the side of his face.

They froze there, breathless, grinning, both of them dusted in white streaks.

Indie tilted her head, her cheeks aching from laughing so much. He looked at her with a softness that made her heart thump against her ribs, something in his eyes that quieted the moment.

Lucas's hands, still coated with flour and butter, came up to cradle her face. She didn't care that he left smudges along her jaw, didn't care that she probably looked ridiculous with flour in her hair and streaks across her nose.

He kissed her, slow and certain, the world narrowing to the warmth of his mouth and the steady strength of his hands holding her as if she were the only thing that mattered. When he pulled back, his forehead rested against hers, his voice low and steady.

"I love you, Indie. I can't wait to spend more days like this with you."

For a moment, she could only stare at him, eyes wide, laughter and tears tangled together in her chest. Then she let out a shaky laugh, brushing her nose against his. "I love you, too, Lucas. Even when you cover me in flour."

He chuckled, kissing her again, quick and firm this time, before pulling away. "Good thing the pie's not done yet, or you'd be wearing that too."

"Don't tempt me," she teased, though her voice was soft.

Together, they shaped the crust and filled it with the blueberries Lucas had picked that morning. Indie snuck a handful into her mouth, pretending innocence when Lucas caught her.

When the pie was in the oven, they stood side by side, fingers entwined, staring at the mess they'd made. Flour coated the kitchen like a blanket, blueberries were scattered on the floor. It was a disaster. A beautiful, perfect disaster.

Indie leaned against his shoulder, her chest full and warm. For the first time, she didn't just feel like she was visiting his world... she felt like she belonged in it.

Later that evening, the house was hushed. The pie was slightly lopsided, edges darker than intended, but fragrant and perfect in its imperfection, resting on the porch railing between them. Lucas cut two uneven slices, handing Indie the larger without comment.

The porch boards were warm beneath their bare feet, and the air hummed with crickets. Fireflies blinked across the tall grass, tiny lanterns rising and falling in the twilight.

"Not bad for our first attempt," Indie said around a mouthful, crumbs catching on her lips.

Lucas leaned back against the post, fork dangling lazily in his hand. "Could use more blueberries."

She laughed, nudging his shoulder with hers. "That's because half of them ended up in my mouth."

"Figures," he said, deadpan, though his lips curved as he looked at her.

For a while, they didn't speak, just ate pie straight from the pan, the sweet-tart blueberries staining their tongues. The quiet was soft, comfortable, and wrapped around them like a blanket.

Indie set her fork down, leaning her head against his shoulder. "You know, if this is what home feels like, I think I could get used to it. If you let me paint a room."

Lucas glanced down at her, his chest tugging in that quiet, certain way. He didn't reply with words, just slid his arm around her shoulders, pulling her closer as another firefly drifted past.

The night deepened, stars pricking the sky one by one. The pie pan sat on the railing, forgotten, as their silence stretched not heavy, not waiting, just two hearts steadying into rhythm together.

Barefoot on the porch, with the taste of blueberries still on their tongues and fireflies flickering like a thousand tiny promises, Indie thought: This is it. This is the life I never knew I was looking for.

And Lucas, with her hand resting over his heartbeat, thought the same.

NICOLE LINETTE

Epilogue

Dancing in the Dark

The house was quiet.

Dinner plates sat in the sink, half-heartedly rinsed, and the soft hum of the dishwasher was the only sign that anyone had been there at all. Indie rubbed her temples as she leaned back on the couch. So much has happened over the last couple of months. She moved into Lucas's house, and her van and trailer sat resting for the first time in a while. Olivia started school, and Charlotte was back running markets. Lucas and her, well, they were learning to ebb and flow with the desire to explore and the tug to stay grounded. She was lost in thought, thinking of their next adventure. Lucas was going to come with her for a short visit to see Eleanor. Indie didn't notice when Lucas slipped out the back door.

It wasn't until he returned, stepping softly into the room, that she looked up. He had that familiar mischievous glint in his eye, the one that always made her suspicious, curious, and warm all at once.

"Come outside with me," he said simply.

She sighed dramatically, but her heart pounded with excitement. She kicked off her shoes and followed him barefoot through the house and out the back door.

The yard had transformed.

Strung between the trees were warm golden fairy lights, swaying gently in the autumn night breeze. They cast a soft glow over the grass, which was still warm from the day's sun. An old radio sat on a small table, crackling to life with a soft, vintage tune as Lucas flipped it on. The kind of music that didn't need words... just slow, crooning instruments that wrapped around you like a memory. The fire pit burned steadily and hypnotically.

Indie stared, a slow smile spreading across her face. "You did all this?"

Lucas didn't answer. He just reached for her hand and gently pulled her closer.

She didn't resist. Didn't say a word.

They began to sway.

There was no choreography. No need for rhythm or even conversation. Just the quiet of the evening, the hum of the music, and the warmth of each other. Her head found his shoulder. His hand settled at her waist.

The world fell away.

Time slowed.

And then, halfway through the song, Lucas leaned close, his breath brushing against her ear.

"This," he murmured, "is what I want every night of my life to feel like."

Indie stilled, heart thudding.

He pulled back just enough to look at her, his eyes soft but certain. His hand reached into his pocket.

"Will you marry me?"

The fairy lights flickered. The music crackled. The air held its breath.

Indie didn't.

She laughed—a breathy, disbelieving kind of laugh and her hands flew to her mouth. Then, with eyes already misted over, she nodded. "Yes. Yes."

Lucas slipped the ring onto her finger with trembling hands. They stood there, in the middle of the yard, under the lights and the stars and the sound of old music, holding each other like it was the only thing they ever wanted to do.

The bang of car doors broke their hypnosis. Indie could hear squeals of joy as Olivia peeled around the corner, her mother close behind, and trailing at a steady pace Hank, Josephine, Sloane, and Eleanor. A sudden shiver shook her from head to toe.

"I told you she would say yes, I told you," Olivia squeezed. Charlotte laughed, sweeping her up into a hug.

"We brought champagne!" Josephine cheered, holding up cups, while Hank lifted the bottles. Indie focused on Sloane walking with Eleanor. This was it, the people she loved, all in one place, every soul who had carved a space in her heart. Her family. Her roots. Her home. She looked up at the sky, blinking back tears, and for the first time in a very long time, she whispered thanks to her mother for sending her people who would forever ground her and fill the void that used to be her heart.

Coming Soon

Wilted Petals & Grounded Roots: The Story of Charlotte Mae Carrington.

Charlotte stood on top of the hill looking out across the field, wild blueberry bushes twisted and tangled together. Peace settled over her skin and weighed heavily on her shoulders. This was going to be her year. She was going to be more than just a member of the Carrington farm.

A horn sounded in the distance, and a shout followed, "Charlotte, let's get going, we can't be late."

A smile bloomed across her lips, and her heart skipped a beat. "I'm coming, Daniel," she called back, turning, racing down the gravel path towards her forever...

Acknowledgements

Somewhere between late night brainstorming, countless cups of coffee, and messages that started with "What if...," this story came to life. While the two of us wrote the words, so many people helped us along the way, and we are incredibly grateful for the support, patience, and encouragement that made this book possible.

First, we want to thank our incredible editor, Ramona Mihai, for their thoughtful guidance, keen eye, and dedication to helping us shape this story into its best possible form. Your insight and encouragement meant more than we can say. We are also so thankful to Megan Jayne Designs for creating a cover that captured the spirit of this book so beautifully.

To our beta readers, thank you for volunteering your time and sharing your thoughts on early drafts of this story.

A special thank you to Roxanna and Manali for reading the manuscript in full and offering thoughtful feedback that helped us strengthen this book.

To our families, thank you for the patience, love, and support you showed us while we worked on this book. Thank you for the extra help with the kids, the late night encouragement, and the understanding when we needed to disappear into writing for a while. Your support and love made this dream possible.

And finally, to our readers. Thank you for taking a chance on this story. We hope Indie and Lucas found a place in your heart, and that their journey reminds you that sometimes the most unexpected places are where we finally find home.

And to each other, thank you for every late night message, every wild idea, and every moment spent building this story together. Writing it with you made the journey even more special.

If you'd like to follow along for future books, behind-the-scenes writing moments, and the occasional chaotic author update, you can find us on Instagram and TikTok @authornicolelinette.